# The Witchin' Moon

written
and
Illustrated
by

## T.R.Hart

# The Witchin' Moon

## Story and Illustrations
## by T.R.Hart

## Copyright 2022

# *The Witchin' Moon*

## By T.R.Hart

## <u>Chapter 1: The Ghost Club</u>

Oct 31st 1919

I set off early on that cold, crisp autumn morning and packed some provisions with the intent of spending a few days camping in beautiful Bucks County, Pennsylvania. Having served in the armed forces in the Great War (though I had never seen any real action), I loaded up my Tin Lizzie with camping supplies and victuals. Then, I gassed the old girl up, and set off for my next assignment. Let me explain. It is important to mention that I work as a reporter for the Philadelphia Inquirer under the pseudonym "Sportin' Jack". My Christian name, being unknown to my readers, is John Francis Doherty, the quiet unassuming son of a bar owner from South Philadelphia. Surely one could not blame me for wanting to create a life dramatically different from my own.

I began journalistic career by reporting on sporting and social events in the Philadelphia area. I was able to convince the local newspapers that there was a need for reporting all of the little goings on and gossip in the neighborhoods to drum up sales. I told the printers turned newspapermen that people wanted to, no, needed to know what was going on in their own neighborhood. Parents wanted to see their kids bragged about for their athletic prowess in print. Others needed to know who died, who was getting married, and so on. Crime, no matter how big or small always sells papers. Quite a number of my earliest articles were translated into Italian for the benefit of that large immigrant community who resided in South Philadelphia. There were also Poles, Ukrainians, and of course, Irish as well, all proud of their heritage. Each was eager to be new citizens of the United States of America and what better way to find out than to buy and read a newspaper. Children of those immigrants read aloud to their proud parents in … English!

I hopped from one job to another until the day my work was noticed by the editor of the Inquirer. He took a liking to me and decided that I would be his "man about town". It was he who bestowed the title of "Sportin' Jack" upon me. In order to keep my identity secret, my column headliner contained the sketch of a stylishly handsome man with a pipe clenched between his teeth, and a trendy fedora with a rakish tilt, adorning that fabulously proud head.

Well, that will suffice for the "History" of John Francis Doherty. I soon grew tired of hopping trolleys, and catching rides with the Police, so it was natural that I sought to purchase a motorcar of my own. As my scope had broadened, I no longer felt confined to downtown "Philly" (No true Philadelphian would call our city anything else) and so, I extended my reach to the more rural areas of Pennsylvania as well. The beautiful autumn colors and fresh cool breezed stimulated my senses and gave me the desire to be outdoors and communing with nature. I decided that an excuse for a getaway from the city was necessary and I thought long and hard about it. Then, it came to me one afternoon as I sat in silence in front of my typewriter.

It is always difficult finding something interesting to write. After spending a considerable amount of time wracking my brain for something new, I finally decided to write an article on ... ghosts! After all, it was the perfect time of the year to do so as Halloween was approaching in a few days from now. I became unnaturally giddy with excitement at the thought of such a preposterous idea... and, what a splendid idea to ask the modern reader! "Do you believe in ghosts?" Could such apparitions still be believed by these "sober-minded" readers? Well, the response was swifter than I could imagine and there were fewer unbelievers than believers. "Sportin' Jack" inquired to meet with anyone with credible stories concerning these disembodied spirits, and I, rather, he (Jack), would not be disappointed.

Letters poured in to the newsroom for "Jack". Many wanted to meet up with him, but a certain letter came to my attention which I believed would give me the seed to a good Halloween tale, and a well-deserved vacation within driving distance. The letter was addressed to Sportin' Jack from a Mr. Latimer Cherry from an address in Bucks County, PA. It stated that if I would be kind enough to accept his invitation and attend the annual festivities celebrated by his Club, that I would surely be convinced that the stories of Ghosts and Goblins were not mere fairy tales but were valid accounts of supernatural encounters. The group was aptly named "The Ghost Club" as each of the members recounts a tale in regards to a world which exists in the shadows of our own and of their own experiences with it.

"What luck!" I mused. This would be the perfect opportunity for an excuse to get away from the office and take a little vacation. October 31st fell on a Monday. Since I spent my weekend covering events in Philly, my editor surely could not deny me this story when all would be quiet around town. I argued my point with logic in a firm, yet non-adversarial tone. My boss was a skinflint and offered little recompense for lodging, to which I replied that I was well-accustomed to roughing it in the outdoors due to my training in the Army. I know this ruffled his feathers a little. You see, few rich men actually fight the battles that the poor boys do. By greasing palms, many wealthy draftees were afforded that special diagnosis that confirmed their inability to serve.

So, looking every bit the refugee, with my Lizzie packed to the gills with provisions and every luxury… and of course, with map in hand, I started off on my journey, convinced that I would attend the little party, jot down some notes for a story and then hurry off to spend the better part of the week fishing, relaxing, and sleeping under the stars. Ah, what a heavenly time I would have!

I made good time that morning, exiting Philly, and travelled on the newly constructed Lincoln Highway which was so smooth that was able to reach a breakneck speed of forty-five miles per hour! At that speed rate I believed that I would arrive much too early to the party, so I decided to pull over onto the side of the road and enjoy my lunch … an Italian sandwich of meat, cheese, and salad all wrapped up into a foot-long roll of bread. The Italian workers would take these familiar sandwiches, which they referred to as "hoagies" to sustain them throughout the work day which was often labor intensive. I decided to wash this sumptuous meal down with an American classic – Coca Cola!

After exiting the highway, I sensed that my luck had taken a turn for the worse having become lost in the labyrinth of small roads that wound through the little towns and farms. These vistas were pleasant enough to view on any other day, but being pressed for time, I feared that I would not arrive at my destination before nightfall. If unable to arrive that day my trip had been in vain, if not perilous, travelling on undeveloped roads cloaked by darkness.

At about 5 o'clock in the afternoon the skies were getting darker and I became somewhat anxious. I finally spotted a man walking down a well-travelled graveled road and in desperation, asked for directions. He was a small, but sturdy looking fellow, and I guessed him to be a farmer or his hired hand. He was friendly enough and impressed with my motorcar, painted dark green and with sporty red pinstripes. Although his directions were somewhat clear, my anxiety grew with the hour approaching and I offered to take him for a ride if he would take me to my destination. He hesitated in a way that I suspected fear in his demeanor. The man politely begged off and pointed in a northerly direction and exclaimed: "Yeah, the house is right ahead mebbe' two miles and then to the left. You won't miss it. It's the only house on the road…strange lookin' too. Well, good luck young man."

The road narrowed. My "Lizzie" was a sturdy little gal, but I was forced to slow down to a crawl as she was jerked around by the uneven ground and nearly ran off of the road. The area was deeply wooded and my visibility was impaired by a swift wind that caused a carpet of dead leaves to rise up in my path. "Perhaps it was one of those small tornadoes referred to as "dust devils" which occasionally appeared I thought. Then suddenly, the wind became stronger still. I escaped certain death when a large branch fell from the most gigantic oak tree that I have ever seen in my life into the path ahead of my car. The shock of this incident caused me to turn sharply and into a ravine. I tried in vain to extricate my motorcar for about a quarter of an hour before I decided that any further attempts would be futile. The Sun descended on the horizon and the sky grew darker and darker. Surely there would be someone in attendance at the Ghost Club who could assist me. And, with that thought in my head, I shouldered my back pack and decided to search for Mr. Cherry's residence.

I walked for a short distance as the sun was setting. I became agitated and my nerves were frayed. So I decided to harken back to my military training and began to march. I sang a dirty little song which always raised a soldier's spirits. It settled my nerves a bit but then, an overwhelming unease came over me when the wind picked up once again and brought a stench of rotting …well… I believe it to have been, pumpkin flesh!

A pumpkin patch laid straight ahead … a promising sight! Surely a house would be nearby, so I followed the darkened path as well as possibly. A shadowy figure stood alone in the patch to my right while a stiff breeze blew in my face filling my nostrils with that most hateful odor encountered moments before.

"Excuse me!" I shouted to the figure. There was no response. I was annoyed and repeated in a louder (and in all probability) angrier tone. "Excuse me!" I cried out once again. The figure turned its face toward me with a menacing look. It was hideous with darkened orbital cavities emitting an eerie glow that shook me with fear. A violent gale blew in my direction and the figure, with the utmost haste, charged toward me, clawing at my arm. By then, I was in abject fear. My heartbeat raced. Spying a lighted house up ahead, my legs moved faster than the quickest stallion as this spook was in hot pursuit of me!

Terrible shrieks and hisses filled the air. I almost stumbled once, but quickly regained my footing. I heard leaves crunching and twigs snapping behind me. The stench of what now seemed to be rotting flesh grew stronger with every second that passed and a flapping sound like the wings not of a bird, but of some horrible winged creature could be heard above me. The seconds that passed while en route to the door of the house seemed like an eternity, but I reached it safely and pounded on it yelling "for Heaven's sake, let me in!" I turned to face my attacker whom I thought would end my existence when the malevolent thing suddenly shot up into the sky and disappeared into the night.

The door opened suddenly and I found myself falling into the arms of a large somber looking man who looked down at me with a grin and said: "Sporting Jack I presume?"

"Mr. Cherry?" I gasped.

"That would be me" he replied. A chorus of subdued laughter and giggling children emanated from within the candlelit room warmed only by a roaring fire in the hearth. "Come this way Mr. Sporting Jack! There are plenty of good victuals and a delicious hot punch to warm yer' bones, pleasant company … and of course, some lovely young ladies waiting for a dance partner."

"Did you see that thing Mr. Cherry?" I gasped.

"No lad, I saw not a thing. You have had a fright. Do have a rest for a minute."

I quickly found the nearest window and looked through it. A large sinister looking moon was rising on the horizon, silhouetting the trees and casting long shadows on the ground. I must have appeared a madman to the guests whose cheerful banter had turned silent. I felt like a coward and truly ashamed for my behavior.

Mr. Cherry clapped his hands together and the sudden silence was interrupted by the ebullient sound of a country fiddler accompanied by a man on a squeezebox. Tapping feet kept time. Laughter and gaiety filled the room. I sipped the drink handed to me from the crowd and detected the presence of some strong spirits. After taking a few draughts from the mug I felt exceedingly calm.

"Feeling better Mr. Jack?" asked a pretty young woman dressed in a beautiful dress and wearing a powdered wig styled in 18th century fashion. Her face was powdered as well and strong rouge applied on her high cheekbones. I could have sworn that I was speaking with Marie Antoinette herself, yet she spoke in perfect English.

"Y-yes… much better, I stammered. Thank you."

"You seemed to have quite a fright. We are so happy that you have accepted our invitation. We feared that you would not come. That would be such a shame."

"I never gave it a second thought. I was so happy to have been invited. Sadly, I did not bring a costume. How foolish of me to forget that this night is All Hallows Eve."

She gave a puzzled look at my response, but smiled, curtsied and took me by the hand and began to dance in that fashion reminiscent of a time long gone by. Try as I might, the steps were complicated and I feared that I might disappoint my partner. She smiled and curtsied once again and I found myself in the company of other revelers.

I have never been to a costume party in which the variety and quality of costume had been assembled. Of course the house was no bigger than an ordinary farmhouse, but in the dim light of that room its walls seem to have expanded into some infinite dimensions. Elegant figures came and went. There were personages from every time period and every place on earth that one could imagine. Romans and Egyptians mingled with American Indians, a Turkish Sultan danced with a New Englander's farmer's daughter, and old Sea Captain intended on charming a medieval lady of some importance. I laughed to myself. These partygoers really played the part to a tee! And so I decided to play the part of Sportin' Jack, American Journalist.

With my notebook and pencil in hand, I began to jot down everything that I could see. What a terrific costume party! I'm was that my readers would love to hear about this annual event! My reception surely had been planned to make a believer of me. Now that I had consumed a couple of mugs filled with punch, my mind settled down. I concluded that I had been the victim of a prank, but now I planned to go along with the ruse.

"Mr. Cherry" I began. "When will the storytelling commence? I am eager to hear them."

"Soon, Mr. Sportin' Jack… I hope you have plenty of pencils and papers. We begin at 7 and end at the stroke of midnight."

I assured him that I did indeed and that I was accustomed to spending entire nights at various soirees and breakfasting afterwards. He chuckled and claimed that I would have my story by then. He sensed that I was an unbeliever and warned me not to go out of the house. I told him that I no longer feared of the "boogey man" that chased me and gave him a wink of the eye.

"For yer' own safety Mr. Sportin' Jack" he said in a most grave tone … "it would be advisable to spend the night.  I protested explaining that my gear was stowed in my motorcar and that I planned camping for a few days.

He shot back with a look that demonstrated to me that he was deadly serious. "Look here, Mr. Sportin' Jack. I would not have invited you had I thought that you were a fool. I'll be warnin' ya for the last time. There's things about in the night that not even the bravest men can stand against. This night is for the old and the evil ones. A sober-minded man will keep indoors where there is safety. They cannot enter these walls. Let them have the night. That light draws them from the grave, the swamp, and the wild woods. Y'see Mr. Sportin' Jack … tonight there be a Witchin' Moon!

## **Chapter 2 – The Chinese Giant**

Before I go on, I should give a brief description of my host. Mr. Cherry is an imposing figure of whom I estimate to stand approximately six feet and a half, or an inch in either direction. The stovepipe hat which he perched upon his large head, gave him the appearance of a giant.  He has a robust physique, despite being considered somewhat portly. His long face is framed with heavy jowls. His nose, large and somewhat reddened, indicated a liking for spirits. Mr. Cherry's voice is deep and resonates as if coming from a vault. His temperament is mercurial, easily irritated and sometimes ebullient but there is no lack of sincerity in his conviction that ghosts do indeed exist. He believes in them wholeheartedly.

Mr. Cherry carries with him a long branch fashioned into a staff that had a thickness that a small man or woman would find extremely difficult to grasp in their hand. The head of the staff is carved into a somewhat grisly death's head and the sound it makes when he hits the wooden floor made a sonorous thud that captures the attention of all present. The room was instantly silent and our host looked up from the brim of his hat which revealed an almost sinister grin. He turned round to the multitude gathered in the room and began to speak:

"Good Ladies and Gentlemen, I would like to welcome you all back once again to our event. It is 7 O'clock and our presentations will begin now. There is an unbeliever amongst us."  A sudden burst of laughter from the members of the "Ghost Club" broke out. Mr. Cherry looked amused and uttered a brief chuckle.

"Now, now" he went on. "Not all of us were believers were we? Some of you, the more sober-minded among us were the most skeptical of all, almost cynics! Our guest here, Mr. "Sportin' Jack, is a skeptic as well, but I do believe that when he has heard your stories, he will become a believer as well. We welcome our guest with open arms. He will hear our stories and record them neither as truth nor lies, but only the words that are spoken. Do your best to remember them as you have heard, or witnessed them yourselves, but our time ends at the stroke of twelve … until next year perhaps when we shall all be together again."

Mr. Cherry looked round the room and from the dim lit corner he called the first of the story tellers to the floor. A small, thin man in oriental attire appeared as if from the ether. His bald head was fringed in white, and his wispy gray beard rendered on to him a most sagacious aura. A large buxom woman in austere black clothing fringed in white lace appeared by his side dwarfing the elderly figure. She introduced herself as Sister Jane Dowd, of the Missions Board of the Presbyterian Church.

"My brothers and sisters, as I was a former Missionary stationed in China for many years and having learned the language, I will be interpreting in English for our honored speaker Mr. De Lung, whose very name translates to "Old Virtuous One". I pray that our Lord will bestow on me his grace to perform my duty to the best of my ability."

A quiet ensued which gave me an opportunity to gather my things together. The old man began to speak in that sing-song style of speaking that is strange to the foreign ear. His voice was low and thin. It was to my advantage that this good woman spoke in a strong and clear voice that conveyed not only the meaning of his words but affected the mood of his story. And now I will relate the old man's story precisely as I had recorded it in my journalist's shorthand:

Many years ago in the land of my birth there lived a poor fisherman and his wife. They lived alone for many years and although they prayed to their gods to give them children, alas, they could have none. So, they went about their lives, worked diligently, and becoming somewhat prosperous, lived a comfortable existence. The wife, however, was still unhappy and yearned to be a mother praying every day for the gods to intercede.

One day as the man was casting his nets, the woman was tending the gardens that surrounded their little home situated on a hill overlooking a small strip of a beach. Just then, she heard a plaintive cry which to her ears was discerned to be a baby! Immediately, she threw down her rake, and began to search the hillside for its source. The cry, which had been stronger earlier, seemed to grow fainter as she desperately looked under each bush, behind every rock, and even into the hollow of a dead tree.

The sun began to set, and the evening star appeared in the sky. The woman stood tiptoed as she scoured the beach with her eyes and finally spotted her husband returning from his day of fishing. She waved her arms wildly and screamed as loud as she could, "Husband, come quickly, I need you!" The husband, fearing that his wife was in danger pulled his boat ashore and ran to her aid. He could see that she was frantically looking for something and thought that she may have lost her reason.

"Wife, what has caused you to act this way?" as he embraced her in an effort to calm her.

"Husband, don't you hear that cry?"

He heard nothing at first, then, heard a muffled crying. "Yes, I do … a baby!"

"We must find it soon as night is falling and it will surely die in the cold of night. The couple searched and searched until finally they came upon the sight of a small bundle of rags. A faint whimper like that of a kitten mewing was heard and the wife ran faster than she had ever run in her life. She bent over and pushed away a pile of leaves, took the bundle up into her arms, and gently lifted the covers. There in her arms was a beautiful little baby! She cradled it as if it were her own and cried tears of joy. "Husband", she declared, "my prayers have been answered. The gods have given us a child!"

The man was happy to see that his wife had not lost her senses and the two made their way home with the foundling. The wife called for her husband to heat some water so that she could bathe the child. Then, she set aside some clean rags for swaddling clothes with which she could bundle the infant to restrain and quiet it while she prepared the bath.

To the disappointment of the husband, the child was found to be …a girl! It was common back in those dark days to leave baby girls to die as they were considered a burden to a poor family. The practice was barbaric to be sure, but the truth cannot be hidden.

"It would have been better to have left the child alone" he muttered in disgust. What good can a girl be to a fisherman? A son could be a comfort in our old age, but a girl?"

The wife became enraged and lashed out at her husband. "And you would leave this child to die? She is a gift from the gods! We, who were without a child, now have been given one to love. It is our duty to raise her, and I will not return her to the wood!"

The husband knew that he had been beaten and asked his wife for her forgiveness. "I will be an honorable father. I give you my solemn oath from this day on. She will be like daughter to me.

As the years went by the infant grew into a beautiful young woman, and yes, she was a comfort to her parents as they passed into their golden years. Her radiant beauty was not only known to her parents, but to everyone who saw her. She was gentle, and the kindness she bestowed on those less fortunate than herself had caused her to be cherished throughout the village.

At about the same time that she was born, there was also born a male infant to another poor fisherman and his wife, and he too was a joy to behold. As a youth he had proven to be an asset to his father as he was an adept with the net as fishermen twice his age. He was fairer than the other boys, somewhat small for his age, but in intelligence he outranked them all, and he too, admired the young maiden named Li Yan, or Beautiful Swallow-bird by her parents who found her in the woods many years ago.

For some time there was happiness in the village. The fish were plentiful and the harvesting had been abundant each year. The villagers were ruled by a wise and benevolent country magistrate, but as he aged there were fears that he would be replaced by a certain official in his court that was known for his cruelty.

The old magistrate did die, and, he died unexpectedly one night To the horror of the villagers he was replaced by a treacherous young man whom many suspected of murdering the old man while he slept. It is reported that when suspicions arose in regards to the death, the new magistrate merely replied that "a pillow is often the cure for one who rests uneasily."

The lives of the villagers changed as if from day to night. Taxes increased at such a rate that many could not pay them. Many of the villagers starved to death rather than incur the wrath of their malicious ruler who extracted every crop, livestock, or coin from them. There were those who never smiled for fear that the gold in their teeth would be discovered … and extracted for payment! Many became homeless and fled to the forest only to find a pitiful existence.

The fishermen worked longer and went further out in their little boats to catch more and more fish until the schools of fish began to disappear. The boy and his father, however, ventured even further than the others, out into the ocean where they knew they could sink their nets into waters filled with schools of fish for their catch.

"See!" The fisherman said to his son. "See how the little fish jump above the waves!"

The boy understood his father as he had seen this many times before. The small fish gathered together in large groups, or shoals, in an attempt to appear larger to the predatory fish. Those on the outer ends of these masses of fish were picked off. Those who managed to get to the center were saved. In their desperate attempt to flee from the larger fish, those in danger leapt from the water. "Where there are little fish jumping, there are big fish lurking" he explained.

Dark clouds began to gather and the fisherman and his little son secured their nets and pulled such a load of fish into the boat that it sank low into the water. Their joy would turn to tragedy however, as the rain began to fall. The father strained at the oars as he struggled to return to the shore while his son took a bucket and desperately bailed water from the bottom. The storm grew in intensity and the little boat creaked and groaned under the weight of their catch. Soon they were in view of the shore but not yet out of danger.

The fisherman's wife stood on the water's edge fretting for the safety of the two as the little boat struggled to stay afloat while still bounding homeward. The waves were rough but the boy jumped from the boat, touched bottom and guided the boat ashore as his father struggled to keep it from capsizing.

"Grab a rope and swim to shore my son to get help!" The fisherman cried as a small crowd of men quickly formed a line from the shore to the boy. One of the men headed into the water. Then each of the men in turn waded out into the water and grasped one hand to the man in front of him and one to the back and thus forming a human chain.

"Boy, give us the line, we will pull you in!" the lead man shouted. The boy's father struggled in the turbulent water as the rain pelted him. He was tiring from his time at the oars and the weight of the boat increased with the deluge that had begun to pour down. The fish began to leap from the little boat into the waters, but there was no time to despair. The fisherman and his son were struggling to keep from drowning.

From out of the sky a streak of lightning cracked and struck the little boat. It exploded into thousands of splinters with such a great boom that the men screamed in fear and let go of the line. A surge of electricity raced down the salty wet line and struck the boy. Though he appeared to be lifeless in the water, one brave man forged ahead and handed his little body from one man, and then to another, and another, and finally into the arms of his grieving mother who had witnessed the horror that had taken place.

Oh the wailing of the mother! Her husband was gone, taken by the waves to his final rest never to be found yet she had not a moment to mourn. She took the boy and covered him with her cloak bringing him close to her body to warm him.  She quickly brought him to their little home as the woman of the town accompanied the wretched woman watching vigil as the boy lay motionless on the bed.

Could it be? One of the women looked on in disbelief as she saw the boys' eyes flutter! Then there was movement in the fingers, followed by a rising and falling of the chest.

"He breathes! He is breathing" She yelled out. The other women turned and witnessed the child breathing normally and resting peacefully. The boy's mother, overcome with joy, rushed to her child and cried out, "He lives, my boy lives! The gods are merciful!"

He slept for several days, but when on waking he behaved like a small child. His body had been spared, but his sharp mind had been dulled by the stroke of lightning. Thankfully his strength increased with each day and the poor woman did her best to make ends meet, but if not for the charity of the people of the village the two would have surely perished from want.

As time went by, the mother noticed something strange happening to her son. Although they lived on a meager diet, the boy began to grow … and grow … and grow! Within a year he had grown a half of a foot taller. With another year he had grown another foot! By the time the boy had become a young man he had grown to be a Giant no less than 8 ft. in height! It was a strange sight indeed to behold as the frail diminutive mother would raise her hand up high to grasp the hand of her son. His face wore a perpetual smile upon it like most imbeciles, but he was cheerful, obedient and possessed a gentle demeanor.

Most of the villagers treated the Giant with kindness, although some of the children would occasionally toss a rotten fruit in his direction or pull some kind of malicious prank on him. It was on one of these days that the Giant was performing an errand for his mother that one of the boys attempted to throw a cabbage at him. The boy raised the cabbage, and just as he was about to let it fly from his hand he felt a strong grip upon his wrist.

"Drop it!" The voice came quick and terse. The boy looked behind him and readied his fist. He was about to strike when he realized it was Li Yan, the beautiful girl rescued from the woods many years ago. He felt foolish and began his lie "I would not hit him Li Yan, I meant only to frighten him." Realizing that he had been caught in a lie, he bowed his head in shame and ran away."

The Giant turned to her with a childish grin and offered her a plum. She thanked him and bit into the most delicious plum that she had ever eaten in her life. Her smile made him laugh in that silly manner that simple minded persons often do. This act of kindness touched her heart and two became fast friends that day. Her beauty and noble manner protected him from those who would make sport of him. She, in turn, became like a daughter to the mother of the Giant, and he became like a son to the parents of Li Yan.

Stories of the Giant's great size and strength soon caught the attention of the evil magistrate. To curry favor with the Emperor, whose tastes for the grotesque and the exotic had filled his court with human oddities, imbeciles, and dwarves; he intended to send the Giant as a gift.

One day as the Giant was pulling a plow through the fields he was approached by the Magistrate's guards. He was told to lay down his plow and come with them immediately, to which he responded with a simple smile, and dutifully followed the men. It was while he was being escorted that the figures of men on horseback and the Giant were silhouetted on the setting Sun. The procession caught the eye of Li Yan who had been desperately searching for the Giant as he has not returned for supper.

For two days and two nights the beautiful Li Yan followed the men with the Giant in tow. Finally they arrived at the courtyard where the Magistrate sat on his throne surrounded by his servants. The Giant, who was unaware of the court protocol, stood facing his lord with a silly smile. The chief of the guard, unaware of the Giant's limited mentality, mistook his demeanor to be disrespectful and gave the poor lad a vicious blow with the flat side of his sword bringing about a deep throated cry from the poor lad. He fell to the ground in pain and lay in a fetal position covering his head in terror.

"Fool!" shouted the Magistrate. "Do nothing to harm the Giant for he is to be a gift for the Emperor!" The head guard, realizing that he would be put to death if anything should happen to the Magistrate's "gift" immediately prostrated himself on the ground and begged for mercy. The Giant, seeing this display, playfully mimicked the guard causing the Magistrate to break out into a fit of laughter.

Unbeknown to those in attendance, Li Yan had witnessed the entire incident by hiding in a tree that overlooked the courtyard wall. "I must rescue the Giant for his mother will be heartbroken, but I must wait until nightfall" The brave young woman waited until all were asleep and slipped into the palace to search for the Giant.

The halls of the great palace were illuminated by many beautifully decorated lanterns which hung in rows on each side of the great stone walls. Silently and stealthily she crept, stopping often when hearing the slightest sound. A soft, deep, muffled cry could be heard from one of the rooms locked behind an iron gate. She tiptoed past several of the sleeping guards until she finally came to the source. It was the Giant! His head was buried in a pillow as he wept softly and called for his mother.

Tears filled the beautiful eyes of Li Wan. "How can I get the key to free my dear friend?" she wondered. "It hangs so high on the wall, and I am so small." Then suddenly an idea popped into her head and a smile crossed her cheeks…she would reach the key with the Giant's help!

"My dear friend" she whispered. "I need your help to get the key so that I may unlock the gate. Stick your arms through the bars and raise me up so that I may retrieve it." The Giant smiled as he beheld his beautiful friend. He did exactly as asked, held his long arms out, and raised her high above the floor. Sweet little Li Yan retrieved the key and within seconds the two quietly crouched low and crawled down the hallway and out of the palace door.

The two fled into the dark woods and hid themselves during the day, but their flight would soon be discovered by a local villager, an evil drunkard, who led the Magistrate's guards to the unfortunate Giant and Li Yan. They were then brought before the evil Magistrate who they thought would surely kill them, but his rage abated and his heart softened at the sight of the beautiful Li Yan. The Giant, oblivious to the danger that they faced, stood beside the young maiden and smiled as gaily as if nothing was wrong.

The Magistrate's heart was smitten to be sure, but there was lust as well. He was determined to have the beautiful young woman as a concubine and would send the Giant to the Emperor to receive favors for his "gift". True, the Magistrate was still a young man, but he had acquired the avarice and deviousness of a devil that had lived a thousand years!

"My dear little swallow-bird" he addressed the young woman. "You need not fear for your friend. I shall make a great man of him. He will be dressed in the finest clothes, and he will eat as would a king."

"Dear Lord" the young woman replied. "My friend is but a simple man who desires neither fine clothes nor food. He is sad and desires only to return to his poor mother who will surely die without him. Please let him return with me."

Having no intention of losing the young woman or his precious gift to the Emperor, the sly Magistrate smiled and promised that he would indeed return the two to their village fed and clothed. "Please accept my hospitality while you are here. I will send for the servants to bathe and feed you." Li Yan, whose innocence led her to believe his treacherous lies, bowed respectfully, and consented to his offer.

That evening the Giant performed great acts of strength as the villagers looked on in awe. There was music and fireworks which delighted Li Yan and the Giant. The Giant was given drink and he became sleepy. The girl was given a drink as well, and when she awoke found herself lying in a luxurious bed. The evil Magistrate had tricked Li Yan with a sleeping potion and had his men take her to his bedroom chamber. The first sight she beheld was the face of the sinister Magistrate hovering above her. He leapt onto her and started to kiss her neck with the intent of ravaging the poor young girl. Waking in terror to this violent attack caused the girl to scream out, but the guards paid no attention to her. Not one of them would risk a painful and slow death for the honor of a poor and simple maiden.

That blood curdling scream from Li Yan woke the Giant who hurried to her defense. The guards attempted to stop the Giant but feared causing him harm, which would lead to their immediate executions. They were whipped around like leaves in a storm, and then strewn about by the Giant's tremendous strength. The Giant ran to the bedchamber door and broke through it. This terrified the Magistrate who yelled for his guards but to no avail. Like a coward he pulled a knife and threatened to kill the girl, but she wriggled away like a little mouse escaping a house cat. The Magistrate desperately swung his dagger from side to side and cut the Giant which caused him to be enraged. A great ccccrrr-ack was heard and the Magistrate's arm went limp. The Giant then hit the man's head with his massive fist so hard that it was caved in by the blow.

The two fled quickly to the woods once again, but an arrow caught the Giant in his heel, causing him great pain as he fell to the ground. Li Yan turned to him, only to see him being surrounded by the guards who poked and tormented him with their lances. The Giant lay still on the ground in a pool of blood. Thinking that he had been mortally wounded, Li Yan ran through the woods toward her home with tears in her eyes. "My friend had given his life for me. I shall return to give him a proper fisherman's burial at sea!"

The Giant, unbeknownst to Li Yan, had not been killed, but he faced a far worse fate. The killing of the Magistrate was a cause of great concern for the ruling class, and so, it was determined that he would suffer the most painful death of all – Lingchi, a slow process of lingering death. The victim would be slowly sliced to death by a thousand cuts, a cruel form of torture and execution used in China before the revolution not long ago.

I will not go into the death of the Giant as it is too horrible to recount. He suffered in extreme agony for the amusement of the populace who came from miles and miles to witness this grotesque spectacle. The chief executioner of the Giant was a man whose personal vengeance caused him great delight in making the grisly scene play out longer than necessary. He further defiled the Giant by feeding his flesh to the guard's dogs. That monster who enacted this inhuman torture was none other than the Chief of the Guards who had become the new Magistrate!

The Emperor, who was old and feeble, would not realize his gift as originally intended. The "gift" would be still arriving in Peking as planned, but the only the bones would be delivered. The new Magistrate ordered that the bones would be placed in an ornate casket. "I will apologize to the Emperor explaining that the Giant had died, and in order to remove the malicious odor of death, the body was boiled and the bones retrieved. "Surely" he wrote to the Emperor, "you will have your Giant for eternity!"

Li Yan returned to the new Magistrate's palace with the Giant's mother and local villagers to retrieve the body for burial at sea as had been wished by all fishermen so that their bodies would nourish the fish that would be netted to feed their families, but, alas, this was not to be. A caravan led by the new Magistrate had already left for a ship sailing for Peking. Li Yan, the mother of the Giant and the little band of villagers returned home heartbroken.

The ship that contained the bones of the Giant left Shanghai harbor with the Magistrate, a contingent of soldiers, and a small crew headed for Tianjin under a cloudless sky. After debarking at the harbor, they would make the journey overland to the Emperor's palace in Peking. The new Magistrate was euphoric, dreaming of the riches and social standing that he would receive for giving such a special "gift" to the Emperor.

The ship's Captain's mood, however, was far different than that of the Magistrate's. As the long casket was lifted aboard the ship, and the contents of that huge box revealed, he fretted that it would be a bad omen to have a dead body aboard. "Surely nothing good could come from the bones of a Giant executed in such a gruesome manner" he thought. Nevertheless, he was compelled to perform his duties as he would on any other voyage though he felt in his heart that something evil was about to occur.

The little ship hugged the coastline and neared a little fishing village not far from where the Giant had lived. The Captain knew the town well and he had been aware of the truth of the Giant's fate. A cold shiver ran down his spine as he observed the clouds suddenly darken. A fierce wind began to blow his sails so violently that he feared that his boat would capsize and sink into the sea. Thinking quickly, he ordered the men to bring the main sail down as the helmsman at the ship's tiller steered toward the open waters lest they be dashed upon the steep cliffs and lost forever under the crashing waves.

The Magistrate's mood had changed from exuberant to abject fear as the ship danced atop massive crests and fell to the blackness below. He believed that the gods had been angered and prayed for forgiveness, but his words were spoken from fear and not remorse. The sky became black as night and the waves rose to such great heights that it was hard to contrast sea from sky.

In a flash, the sky rumbled and a bolt of lightning hit the mast and traveled down the wetted lines to the deck causing the casket upon it to burst with a tremendous explosion revealing the bones of the

Giant! As the Captain struggled to keep his ship afloat, he prayed aloud to the gods to spare the lives of the crew. From the casket a great and deep bellowing shook each man to his marrow of his spine. It was then that the men beheld a ghastly spectacle take place before their eyes!

The bones of the Giant began to rise up slowly and deliberately from its deathly ensconce. The skeleton fastened itself together, bone by bone, and stood up to its full height and turned menacingly toward all aboard the deck. The skull's sockets burned with a light so bright that it appeared as if a fire had been lit within its recesses. Its jaws moved from side to side and gaped so wide that the mouth appeared as if it were a dark cavern. The sailors were panicked with fear and some jumped from the ship to a certain watery death rather than face the menacing demon that gnashed its teeth and howled like a ravenous wolf. Others recoiled, terrified as if turned to stone, unable to move from the spot where they stood.

The Captain shouted "please spare the lives of my men and show them pity as they have done you no harm!" Its Jaw hung wide, and the head scanned the ship as if looking for something lost. The bones walked the deck menacingly, yet it harmed none in its path. Searching, searching, and then unexpectedly the huge skeletal hand ripped back some canvas and revealed the prostrate form of the new Magistrate, the former chief of the guards. Here was that same swaggering villain who took pleasure in tormenting the Giant in his last moments of life, begging for mercy though he gave none.

The colossal phantom moved slowly toward the fleeing man who screamed in fear as he climbed a line toward the top of the mast in an attempt to escape his grisly fate. The Giant pulled and jerked the line like a cat playing with a mouse. Its jaws hung open wide as if laughing at his prey. The Magistrate held on for his life but as his strength gave way to his weight, he knew that it would be to no avail. Rather than being ripped to shreds as he had done to the Giant he leapt into the sea and found a watery grave.

The Giant then moved toward the gunwales and climbed on top as holding line in one hand. He then turned toward the terrified men. The lights in his eyes grew dimmer and dimmer until they were extinguished. He made no sound and leaned backward. A great rustling was heard as the bones crashed into the waves. The Giant joined his father and all of those before him who toiled in the sea.

Li Yan, whose virtue exceeded her beauty in her later years, never forgot the bounty from the sea the year that the bones of the Giant had returned to its proper resting place. She grew old and wrinkled and recounted the story to her children, and their children, the story which I have told you on this night.

A thunderous applause rose in the crowded room. Mr. Cherry thanked the "Old Virtuous One" De Lung and profusely praised Sister Jane for her gift of translating the story. This, of course, brought a slight blush to this god-fearing woman's otherwise ghostly pallor.

## <u>Chapter 3– The Alehouse Wife's Tale</u>

Bang! Mr. Cherry's staff made a thunderous sound on the planks of the thick timbered floor and gathered the attention of the garrulous guests with its tremendous reverberation. "Whom of you would like to tell your tale next?" he inquired. An immediate reply came from an old crone seated next to the fire. She was dressed from head to toe in brown and black and her round face was topped with a coned hat, which I have to say, gave her the appearance of a witch!

She was not plump, no, she was extremely fat. Her cheeks were puffed so that her eyes appeared to be sunken into them. Her nose was long and sharply pointed with a large wart near the tip. Her voice, rather thin and reedy was voluble enough to be heard as the room had become deadly silent.

"I know that I ain't a pretty bird" she exclaimed with a cackle. "That is how it is with all alewives. The pretty ones watered the beer. I give ye your money's worth." It was true that alewives by law could not be less than 40 years in age at that time. This woman knew her history for sure, but of course, she couldn't fool a cynic like me. Her disguise was quite impressive I thought, so I sharpened my pencil and began to jot down every word that came from her wrinkled lips.

"I heard many stories from loose lips" she began. "In my business it doesn't take long for the ale to work its magic, but there is one that I heard repeated so many times by so many, men and women alike, that I know it to be true. I shall recount it as I have heard it."

This is *her* story:

Many years ago the last year an infamous era of New England came to an end in 1693. It was not uncommon back in those days for neighbors to declare that witchcraft was being practiced under the noses of their leaders by certain individuals with devious intent. If your child became sick, a cow died, or a crop failed, it was quite convenient to blame someone that you had a quarrel with for your

misfortune. Rarely did it amount to more than an admonishment or a short time in the stocks or imprisonment, but people had indeed suffered the ultimate penalty of death…true!

In a little village near Salem, Massachusetts there lived two neighbors, the Winthrops, and the Hopkins. Dred Winthrop, (Baptized "Dread not the Evil One") lived with his pretty little wife Patience, a godly woman. Together they farmed a small piece of land, raised chickens and sold eggs, milk, and butter to the local community, but alas, there was sadness between them. Despite Patience's daily prayers, she was unable to conceive and bear children.

Joseph and Rachel Hopkins, their neighbors, were farmers as well, and eked out a living selling vegetables and milk from the solitary cow which they owned. Joseph was an amiable man who could work wood and stone and was handy at fixing anything brought to him. He was fortunate to have married a sensible and thrifty wife like Rachel, a short, stocky woman with good judgment and business sense, unlike Joseph who would often provide his services without fee. Their family, in contrast to the Winthrop's was quite prolific, having no less than 13 children, and all in good health.

Dred was the son of a well-to-do clergyman and scholar, the Reverend Winthrop. His ancestry included many of the earliest puritan settlers bearing the prestigious name of Winthrop. As a youth he was a handsome roustabout and had captured the hearts of the local young maidens, but it was his wife Patience, a virtuous young woman, who was the favorite of the elder Winthrop who decided that she alone, could bring his son to his senses and settle down to a respectable life.

The young couple was mutually attracted to each other, something of opposites attracting, and were married. Her dowry was small, but adequate and Dred had come into a comfortable inheritance as a result of the decease of both parents. It was not long before Dred had returned to a dissolute life of drink and began to abuse to his little wife, whom he shamefully referred to as the "Barren" Mrs.

Winthrop! She became lonely and so, Patience, bereft of friend and family, sought out the companionship of her neighbor, Rachel. The two became fast friends and conversed with each other daily as they performed their duties: washing, preparing food, and discussing Bible verses. Dred, however, remained aloof, declaring that he would not lower himself to keeping company with uneducated rustics.

Although Dred was dismissive of the Hopkins, he was not so proud to request their services, which were often, and unreciprocated. One day while Patience was feeding their horse, she noticed that it was beginning to develop a limp. Such problems could become much worse if not attended to. Dred, who had grown up without having any practical knowledge, cursed and began to beat the poor animal. Rachel, having witnessed this cruel act, offered the services of her husband to her friend Patience without pay! Joseph immediately diagnosed the problem … The shoe of the horse had broken. It had begun to dig into the hoof of the poor animal and had caused it severe pain, thus causing the limp.

Joseph removed the offending shoe, shaved the hoof down, and began to replace it with another, when Dred entered the barn in a drunken rage demanding to know why Joseph was alone with his wife. Joseph unwittingly turned to face his accuser when the horse, whose foot was in his hand, bucked and kicked the poor man on the side of his head. Patience ran to Rachel and her children who came at once to render aid to Joseph, but alas, he lay dead in a pool of blood. Dred, whose outburst had caused the death of poor Joseph, had already retreated to the house and lay dead drunk on his bed.

Joseph's death was a terrible blow to his family, but the sorrow did not end. There came a sickness that carried off the two youngest of Rachel's children, and afterwards, a crop failure which produced only a meager harvest for the following year. As she was unable to feed all of the children, Rachel relented and allowed her older children to be farmed out as laborers. Times were indeed desperate for the Hopkins!

Dred, despite his shortcomings, had found fortune in the raising of pigs. It was a dirty, smelly job, a life that no Winthrop would ever consider, but times, as mentioned before were difficult. A normal man would have been grateful for his success, but Dred was a vain and greedy man whose newly acquired wealth only fed his ambition to own more, and more land; and that land he wanted the most was the land which was stubbornly held. That land belonged to Rachel Hopkins.

There was a small stream of clear fresh water that ran through the Hopkins's land which Dred wanted an easy access to. As he was extremely tightfisted, he offered no recompense to have water for his pigs, but instead drove them through Rachel's garden for them to drink. There were times that his pigs dug and ate the root crops causing friction between the two. Fences proved no match for the hungry pigs either. To make matters worse, Rachel's complaints fell upon deaf ears as Dred was well connected to the local authorities. His solution seemed quite reasonable to them. Dred explained that he had offered to buy the land, yet Rachel had been obstinate and refused his generous offer.

The offer, of course, was not generous. The land was worth far more than the paltry sum offered by the insatiable Dred Winthrop. Rachel, , was not a member of good standing in the church due to her outspoken manner. The elders agreed privately that it would be advantageous for the goodly people in the village to be rid of Rachel Hopkins once and for all. "After all" remarked the Preacher, "Goody Hopkins was never grateful for the remonstrance given to her when she bemoaned her troubles. Be as Job!" he counseled. "Ye be of good faith and accept the trials for your sins!"

Rachel had not responded well. In fact, she merely pointed out that the Preacher had grown quite fat, and reminded him of the sin of gluttony. The women of the town had no affection for her as well and completely forgot the kindness of Joseph who toiled for the greater glory of God rather than asking for their monies. He was content to accept the prayers for his family which they had promised to keep. "It is easier to put your hands together to pray than to offer a hand to one in need!" Rachel reminded them.

While Dred sought the company of others (women included) Patience was left home alone. Dred forbade her to keep company with the hated Rachel Hopkins and she became lonely once again, bereft of children to give her joy. There were many times when she prayed to God to take her home to his Heavenly kingdom, but alas, she received no answer to her pleadings. Rachel missed her friend greatly, but fearing that Dred would harm Patience, she kept her distance. It was a sad time for both women.

Dred continued to prosper in business and he grew wealthier still. He bought the finest clothes and grew fat by eating rich food but alas, for his beleaguered wife Patience, he was a miser. She was clad in the most ragged attire and grew thin and haggard as scraps of food alone were available. Her husband's words were harsh and his demands upon her became greater, but the greatest wound was that she was "barren" and that no matter how rich they became, he would have no heir. There were the occasional outbursts of defiance from Patience, of course, but these were quickly silenced by a swift backhand across her face.

It was on one of these evenings that Dred had come home exceedingly drunk and querulous. Patience had known that he had been in the company of low women and protested. Dred rose from his stupor and struck her in anger, commanding her to remove his muddy boots. Fearing his wrath, she dutifully removed the boots and hid them before putting him to bed; then she fled from the house with her precious few belongings.

A knock came on the door of the Hopkins's house. Rachel was alone with two of her youngest children. She called out fearfully "Who beckons at this hour?"

"It is I Rachel! Please let me in. I fear that Dred will awaken and search for me."

The door was opened and there stood Patience. Rachel was shocked to see pretty little Patience in such a sorry state. She was so thin that her skin stretched over bone. Rachel was ragged, bloodied, and bruised. "What can I do Rachel? I fear that someday he may take me life, little that it is worth."

"Come in my child. I promise that no harm shall come to thee."

The two women talked while sipping hot tea and eating boiled potatoes. Patience revealed the horrors that she had suffered as a result of her husband's violent temper. What could she do? Surely she had nowhere to go. Patience had neither family nor friend … but Rachel had a plan:

A merchant was coming the very next morning to buy a wagon load of apples from Rachel. It was well known by those who made hard cider, which her apples, tart but sweet, were among the best for that hearty drink. The two agreed that Patience would ride with the man to the neighboring town where Rachel's daughter had found employment. Upon arriving, Patience would seek out the young woman and there she would remain, safe from her abusive husband.

Patience Winthrop's disappearance caused many tongues "a wagging" in that little puritan community. Malicious stories of adultery between Patience and a married man circulated in the little village. This story seems to have originated from one of Dred's paramours whose marital designs on him went unrequited. Then, there were those who believed that unnatural circumstances were involved. Surely the "Evil One" had been making the rounds in Salem where once godly women, now confirmed as witches, had been seduced into his service. Suspicion fell on Rachel as well, accused by the embarrassed and devious Dred Winthrop who now devised a devious plot to confiscate her property.

The friendship between Rachel and Patience had always been a thorn in the side of Dred Winthrop. He remarked that his wife was under the influence of this strong willed busybody of a neighbor. "What nonsense had she filled my wife's head with?" he groaned.

"Since the death of Joseph the woman dresses completely in black, wears a peaked cap under her conical hat, to signify that she is indeed, a widow. "…and with her looks, she'll remain a widow!" he scowled.

Dred managed to arouse sympathy for his plight by exhibiting a mournful, humble, and pious façade to the satisfaction of his fellow congregants. This ruse had caught the eye of the spinsters and suitable widows who were unaware of his true nature. Dred had also dropped hints at the goings on at the Hopkins house now that Joseph was dead and the children gone. Could Rachel have entertained the Evil One in a lustful manner? He made no accusations, but the bitter seeds he planted in their curiosity would bear poison fruit. It would be just a matter of time before Rachel Hopkins would be accused of witchcraft for the spiriting away of Patience Winthrop under the darkness of night.

Still, Rachel stubbornly held on to her land, working the fields as best that she could, raising chickens for their eggs, and finally selling the cow that had provided her family with milk and butter for many years. She had grown frightfully thin, her clothes threadbare, and Rachel's teeth began to rot in her head. Her back was now bowed such that she looked like a witch stirring her cauldron, as she took in work as a laundress for the wealthy, thus providing a steady income.

One night, as Rachel lay on her bed, exhausted from her labors which were too arduous for a woman her age, a knock came on the door. "Rachel Hopkins!" the stern voice of a man bellowed. "Rachel Hopkins answer or we shall break thy door down!" The terrified woman leapt to her feet and let the owner of the voice in.

The familiar voice was that of the Preacher whose gluttony had been admonished by the outspoken Rachel. "Ye are charged with the crime of witchcraft and consorting with the Devil. Thou shalt be tried before the most prudent of men!"

Governor Phips chose men for Rachel's trial whom he described as "persons of the best character and of the highest morals." Among those men were wealthy merchants and high ranking militia officers, nine in all. The chief justice, newly appointed deputy governor of the colony, was joined by three justices from Salem, two from Essex County, and four judges from neighboring Boston, most notably the Major-General Waite ***Winthrop***!

Rachel's heart sank, realizing that she had already been condemned in the eyes of the Church, but she stayed true to her convictions and faced her accusers bravely, ready to die before submitting to their treachery. The trial was a mockery. Rachel stated her case but to no avail. Dred watched the drama unfold and said nothing. In two days Rachel would swing on the gallows with four other unfortunate women whose confessions made under duress would save their souls, but it was still not enough to save their lives.

The poor women suffered the indignation of those in the village who took a malicious delight in tormenting them, but most of the insults were directed at Rachel, the witch who had spirited away Patience Winthrop. On the night before the women were to be hung, Dred Winthrop went to see his beleaguered victim. His cool demeanor, along with his feigned piety, brought out a tirade from the accused witch.

"Ye know that I am but no witch Dred Winthrop! There be no sorcery in the disappearance of thy wife! It is ye who caused her to flee in the night. It was ye who beat her black and blue. Thy piety is but a mask that you wear to hide thy face. In truth, ye are but a blackguard. It is my land that you coveted, though ye had plenty. A curse be on ye! A pig thou art and a pig thou shalt be!"

Rachel had sealed her fate with those words spoken in anger. A sly smile was the only response given by her tormenter. Dred then looked about him and gave a look upward as if to be praying to God almighty. That devil, Dred Winthrop, had won at last! The land which he coveted would now be his. A paltry gift to the congregation was all that was needed for Rachel's land. No other persons would even consider owning the land that belonged to a witch!

Dred went home that evening feeling quite happy with himself. Having no conscience, he felt nothing of the injustice which had been levied on poor Rachel. Of course, he would not live on the land, but rather a poor widow with child would benefit from his kindness. She lived in the Hopkins's house, and being the pious soul that he was, Dred decided that he would visit them often …especially at night when the child was fast asleep.

The day of reckoning had finally come for Rachel and the other witches. A large crowd gathered round, and food had been prepared for the festivities that followed. The judges had been prudent to have been able to find every one of the witches to be guilty. And, of course, it may not have been possible without the strong influence of Major-General Wait Winthrop to convict the hated Rachel Hopkins.

Dred was in a giddy mood, but was shrewd enough to conceal his mirth.  Completely dressed in black, and wearing a prominent black tie, the sign of a grieving widower, his tall figure attracted admiration from the young women, and pity from the elders.

The time drew near. The jailer, a large oaf of a man, made his way to the dark and dingy cell which contained the poor wretches. One by one the women were led to the gallows. But what was this? There were only four women! Where was Rachel Hopkins? He counted four on his fat fingers… and then once more. Only four! Rachel was nowhere to be found. "Surely she could not have escaped" he gasped. The lock had been untouched. Had he unlocked the door himself? The question ran through his simpleton's mind. "Yes, I will tell them that she bewitched me!"

Days and weeks passed following the execution of the "Witches", but still there was no sight of Rachel. There were two theories in regards to her disappearance. Perhaps she had been saved by God Almighty and had indeed been innocent. "No!" others responded. "Surely she was guilty and was spirited away in the night by a demon!" Nevertheless, Dred ignored the gossip and returned to the life he knew. True to his word he kept company with the poor widow whose son bore a close resemblance to Squire Dred Winthrop.

During this time, Dred had begun to put on an appreciable amount of weight. He had been used to eating fine foods and was notorious for his fondness for sweets. Although he dressed in the finest clothes, he noticed that he no longer attracted the attention of the pretty young women in the village. Each morning as he dressed in front of the looking glass, he began to notice changes in his appearance.

"My, oh my, the cheeks grow fat. Perhaps I shall eat less of the sweets!" There were other changes too. Dred's clothes grew tight about his waist. The nails on his fingers and toes became so thick that he was obliged to cut them with a sharp knife several times a week. There were changes in his mannerisms as well. Dred's voice became quite deep and his speech was punctuated by noticeable grunts and it was not long before he noticed that others in the village found him to be repulsive. They began to question his relationship with the "widow", and now avoided his company altogether. No matter how little food he consumed, or tried to groom himself, he became fatter and more uncouth as the mirror would reveal.

As time passed by, Dred became lonely for the company of his friends. The "Widow" who had welcomed his nighttime dalliances in the past, grew cold and distant to her former lover. One night she rejected him altogether and claimed that his hideous form could no longer be tolerated. On the very next night he found the door locked and bolted. When he went the next day to speak his mind about her erratic "behavior" he was greeted by an open door ... but there was no one inside. The "Widow" and her son had left town without a word. Dred now felt totally alone.

Dred took once again to drink. He wallowed in self-pity, let his house go to ruin, and cared little for his personal cleanliness. Still, each morning, he dressed in front of his mirror and was shocked by his appearance. Could it be that his ears grew long and pointy? Was his nose growing longer, fatter, and turning upward? Then suddenly he remembered the words uttered by Rachel Hopkins as she awaited her fate: "A curse be on ye! A pig thou art and a pig thou shalt be!"

"She has cast a spell upon me!" he cried. He could not be seen in this sorry state. "That Witch has cast an evil spell upon me. I must seek the counsel of the Preacher to lift this curse from me." Dred looked around the room frantically for the largest cape he could find. He hid his face behind a large scarf and upon his head he placed a wide brimmed hat and plucked the feather from it in an attempt to hide his former vanity. He waited until sundown ashamed to be seen, then made his way to the Preacher's house and knocked on the door.

"Who comes knocking at this time of night?" asked a voice from within.

"It is I, good Reverend, Dred Winthrop!"

"I know thee not, but ye are welcome."

The door opened and Dred slowly walked past the Preacher who seemed startled by the strange clad figure. As he turned to face his host he realized that this was not the old, fat Preacher, but rather a young man, pale and thin, and unknown to him. He was told that the old preacher had been struck with a severe pain to the stomach, had lingered for some days, and then went to be with "God in Heaven above", but the truth was that his gluttony had proved to be his undoing. Following the feasting which commenced after the hangings, he had eaten so much that his stomach burst. An infection ensued which caused him to fever. It can be noted that in his delirium he had uttered the most unholy language ever heard from a clergyman!

"Preacher, I am a sinner" Dred testified. "I have done wrong to be sure, but it is only because I have been bewitched! Pray thou for me that I may quit this hideous form!"

The Preacher said a prayer for Dred and begged God to cast the evil curse from him. Dred thanked the man, dropped a small bag of gold into the palm of the preacher's hand and then departed for home.

Dred woke the next day feeling that his soul was cleansed and that God would smile upon him once again. "Surely my gift was a good thing" he mused. I shall do good from now on and my life will be as it was before." But the Lord Almighty knows when the heart is contrite and when the fox is at play… Dred slowly walked up to the mirror, raised his eyes, and to his horror saw the image that he feared… he had become a pig!"

Dred squealed in terror and ran from his home. He began to seek the company of his pigs and like them began to grovel in the dirt and mud. The other pigs furiously turned on him and began to tear at him until he took his last breath. Dred Winthrop was dead! He died as he lived…as a pig!

"There be a lesson to be learned" cautioned the Preacher in his sermon. "Though a man has riches, the greatest gift to him is God's grace. Without it and the fellowship of man, he is nothing but the dirt from whence he came."

The Alehouse wife concluded her story: "Dred Winthrop's burial was plain and simple. His torn body was that of a man and not a pig. It was, by his own reckoning that the curse came true. It was not by Rachel's words, but, by his deeds alone."

As I jotted down the last words of her story, I lifted my eyes to her that I may ask a question, but alas, she was gone, and the next storyteller stepped into the light.

## <u>Chapter 4 – The Boatswain Mate's Tale</u>

Standing next to the fireplace lighting his pipe, was a burly young man in sailor's attire which I reckoned to be from the early nineteenth century. His horizontally striped shirt revealed a broad chest underneath. A scarf was tied 'round his neck, and a wide brim hat of straw hung loosely on his shoulders. It was tied in a bow as one would tie their shoelaces below his jaw. Since a sailor made a pittance for his labors, the cost of a hat could set him back a small fortune. A stiff wind could send it as a gift to Neptune and thus deprive its wearer protection from the blinding rays and the heat of a noonday Sun.

The wind outside moaned and blew with a ferocity that caused the young man to rap on the window. He held a fist to an imaginary foe one the other side of the glass and declared: "Shut yer trap, or I'll close it fer ye!"

As he came into the light I was able to get a good look at him. He was of middling height, very broad-shouldered, and with the thinnest waist giving him the physique of a Grecian statue. He was, perhaps, between from twenty to twenty and five years. His hair was black and curly with a pigtail held in place with a lump of tar (excellent touch in keeping with accuracy). In fact, sailors were known as "Jack Tars" for this habit … and the scarf? Well it was necessary accessory for his outfit if the sailor wanted to keep the tar from soiling his shirt collar.

He stuffed his clay pipe with tobacco once again and lit it with a twig which he had deftly put into the fire. After drawing in several strong puffs into his lungs, the handsome young man commenced to launch smoke rings into the air. This little trick was greatly appreciated by the children who expressed their delight with "oohs" and "aahs". I do believe that I heard giggles come from the young ladies as well.

"It's lovely to be back on terra firma again" the sailor began. "It's been so long since me feet have stood still that I don't think that I

can stand still!" He then performed a little jig with his hands fixed firmly on his hips. The piper was quick to accompany him on his pennywhistle as the crowd moved to and fro in the dimly lit room clapping and cheering as the young man expertly performed this seaman's frolicking. He feigned exhaustion and said: "Well, me feet have been satisfied, now it's time for me story. Do ye all want to hear a yarn?" The crowd replied with a resounding "Yeah!"

The story began with three characters; the ship's naturalist, a young midshipman, and a boatswain from a ship that sounded quite familiar to me. He stated that the HMS Beagle mentioned was indeed that very ship made of renown of the famous, or infamous scientist, (depending on your position on that controversial Theory of Evolution) Mr. Charles Darwin. I questioned him if the naturalist of whom he spoke was the same Mr. Darwin. He answered in the negative and explained that the story that he was about to tell took place ten years before that historic journey.

HMS Beagle was launched in 1820, thirteen years before the voyage of discovery that gave the ship its everlasting fame. It was a small two-mast vessel of about 90 feet. Its main function was that of a supply ship, but its smaller size, and subsequent lower draught made it quite adept for navigating closer to shore to take "soundings", which is the measuring of the depth of the water from the surface to the ocean floor. This was essential for determining whether the water was deep enough for harboring, or if dangerous reefs hidden below the water would split the ship's hull in two.

The three men from the Beagle, mentioned before, were in small dinghy, taking these soundings close to the shore of a small strip of land situated nearby Fiji Island. Midshipman Josiah Hampton Simms was a mere lad of 16 years, Bo' sun's mate Johnny Burke, 25 years of age, was manning the oars, and directing the two was the ship's naturalist Mr. Stewart Campbell, a civilian who was approaching the half century mark, but appeared much older.

"Mr. Simms, your reading?" Campbell inquired authoritatively.

"Reading - 40 ft. sir" he responded…"Plenty of depth to take harbor." Campbell, ignored his assessment, jotted down the reading, and then gave the order for the boatswain to row ten feet closer to the shore. The readings however indicated that the reef was very dangerous as some readings were deep enough to harbor a vessel, yet a mere ten foot away could be less than ten feet which was much too shallow.

"Coral can create a labyrinth below the waters Mr. Simms" the naturalist lectured. "We cannot assume anything, but by taking many soundings we can save the lives of many whose unsuspecting captain might dash his ship to pieces on these reefs!" The embarrassed young man responded in a little more than a whisper, while the burly boatswain smiled broadly and swung the boat around for the next sounding.

"Sir, we might be getting back to the ship as the sky is looking a wee bit dark."

Mr. Campbell was too busy taking notes to respond to Johnny Burke's advice. Midshipman Simms, who had been admonished for his premature assessment, was too intimidated to point out the darkening clouds that were approaching them. The minutes seemed like hours as Campbell continued to ignore the impending threat.

Suddenly the wind blew up enough fury to make Campbell take notice. The waves began to swell and the naturalist had decided too late to make his way back to the ship. Burke struggled at the oars, but to no avail. The Beagle, fearing proximity to the island without knowing it to be safe or dangerous, made the prudent choice to drop its main sail and head for deeper water. As the ship faded from view the men's hearts sank, but now the struggle was had begun to save their lives.

"Quickly…row to shore!" Simms ordered.

"Aye, aye sir!" Burke replied. Campbell clutched his notebook and shoved it in his shirt. All looked out in horror as the waves threatened to capsize them at any moment.

With a herculean effort Johnny Burke pulled on the oars. As he strained with all of his might, there were times that he could hear the boat scrape violently upon a reef and he feared that the dinghy would come apart at a distance too far from shore. Still, the boatswain pressed on despite the growing strength of the wind and quickening of the current pulling them down to an unknown fate.

Water washed over the sides of the little boat. Simms and Campbell bailed furiously to keep her afloat, but alas, it was to no avail as the dingy sank lower and lower in the water. Johnny managed to get 20 yards from shore when the boat began to splinter.

"It's best to make our way from here. Jump out and swim for your lives!" Campbell screamed in terror. Burke held steady while the others jumped into the water and made their way toward the shore. There were times that the men thought that the sea would carry them out to their deaths, but slowly and surely they groped their way among the coral and made their way to the shore.

Johnny struggled at the oars desperately trying to bring the boat in while Simms and Campbell, now safely ashore, looked back in horror. The dinghy was rocked and buffeted by treacherous waves. The Bo 'sun's strength was being sapped with every passing second and then came the final blow! The dinghy broke in two. Johnny dived beneath the water and found a semi-submerged reef to hold onto. He was head and shoulders above the waves for a few moments and then completely submerged beneath them the next, but he grabbed and hugged his way closer and closer to safety. He was just about to make land when he was overcome by fatigue and then the lights went out.

Johnny Burke woke to a familiar sound. Was he dead or alive? He could see light above, yet the images he saw were blurred. It was then that he heard the commanding voice of Campbell who stood over him. He was slapping his face in an effort to revive him.

"Burke, Burke, can you hear me?"

Johnny was groggy yet quick enough to grab the hand that was slapping on his cheek. "Thank the Almighty Mr. Simms. Mr. Burke is among the living!"

## <u>Cannibals!</u>

The men's joy soon turned to anxiety as they realized the seriousness of their situation. Would they ever be rescued? Still, they made the best of their situation and began for forage for food, but the most immediate concern was to find a source of fresh water.

Unable to find a source of potable water on their new home, it was suggested by Mr. Campbell that the abundance of fresh fruit would serve them well for liquid refreshment. This liquid was ubiquitous on the island in the form of "Cocos Nucifera", better known to the layman as Coconut Palm trees.

"Lads, have you ever tasted coconut milk? It is quite nutritious and tasty I might add" Campbell asked the men. Of course, the reply was in the affirmative. Coconuts had been gathered before each departure. It was easy to store, it did not spoil so easily as the water, and its meat could be prepared in various ways or eaten from the nut.

"We must procure them for our very survival" he added. Of course the task was to fall to someone athletic enough to climb the trees to gather the fresh coconuts and it would certainly was not Mr. Campbell, approaching fifty and with a noticeable paunch brought on by a sedentary life of scholarly pursuits.

Johnny Burke offered, but as he was still weak from his exertions which had almost cost him his life, he was quickly overruled by Mr. Simms who gamely offered to do the job himself. And so, on the following morning, the young officer set off to gather coconuts.

The task proved to be much more difficult than he had anticipated. Josiah Hampton Simms was adept at "climbing the ropes" up to the highest crow's nests and it might be noted that he bravely performed that feat in one of the most violent tempests known to his crew… but scaling a tree without branches was an entirely new and difficult technique to accomplice for the novice tree climber. As he was determined to accomplish his task, he finally succeeded in shimmying up the palm in about an hour of initiating his first attempt.

The desired fruit was directly above him. Simms produced a small pocket knife and began to cut the stem of the fruit. This knife, given to him as a boy by his father, had served him well, and now it would be useful in saving his life.

Mr. Simms easily cut the stems while holding firm to the tree. One by one the coconuts fell to the ground with an audible "thump". It was the distinct crashing sound of a falling coconut which brought his attention to the stirrings of something beneath him. To his horror the young man witnessed a congregation of large crabs gathering at the base of the tree. One had been smashed to pieces by the falling coconut.

He ceased working immediately and began to yell out for help, but there was no reply. Sweat poured down his face. He was weary and wondered how much longer his arms could hold onto the tree. Just when he thought his situation could not become worse he saw the largest of the crabs ascending the very tree that he was on.

Mr. Campbell, occupied in determining the best strategy for their survival, was milling about the shore while Johnny Burke took a well-deserved rest. A high pitched scream, first thought to be a woman in peril, startled the men to attention. They ran quickly to the source of the commotion only to find the unfortunate Mr. Simms hanging onto the palm tree in terror being besieged by a large gathering of Coconut-Crabs tearing away at their meal.

Campbell and Burke restrained themselves from laughing at the poor unfortunate Simms, the perpetrator of the girlish scream, and began the process of extricating him from his plight. Burke took a malicious delight in smashing the crabs indiscriminately as he made his way toward the young officer, until he was stopped by Mr. Campbell who regarded this wanton destruction of such fascinating creatures as cruel and barbaric.

Campbell reasoned that the crabs were a tasty option for a meal, readily available, and it would take some time to fashion a net or even a hook and line to catch fish that came and went with the tide. Johnny Burke offered that he indeed could fashion the necessary items from the sounding line which Mr. Campbell had in his coat pocket and any metal that he could hammer into shape.

It was during this commotion that the three castaways were spotted by a heavily tattooed native who had been fishing from his canoe. As he started to paddle his boat away from the island, the Boatswain leaped in the water and swam after him in an attempt to keep him from revealing the location of the castaways to the cannibals.

The frightened man paddled for his life and eluded capture. Realizing the futility of his efforts, Burke returned to the others shouting and cursing their misfortune.

"Bloody Hell, we are doomed men. He will bring his friends back to do us harm!" lamented Campbell

"We could find safety in the Jungle?" the midshipman inquired.

"It'll do no good Mr. Simms. The Island is scarcely a square mile. They would find us in no time" replied a defeated and desolate Mr. Campbell.

Johnny Burke, still reeling in anger would have none of Campbell's pessimism. "Hide? Give up? Not I! I will fight to my very last breath rather than to be a willing feast for the savages! We will prepare to defend ourselves and our island!"

Campbell and Simms, lacking Johnny's brawny limbs and fiery resolve, resigned themselves to fight, no matter how futile it may be, under the leadership of the fearless Bo'sun.

Nightfall came, yet the men continued their preparations for the anticipated assault on their little island kingdom. "General", Johnny Burke, took inventory of all their weapons including those in a hastily fashioned redoubt that was filled with anything that could be used as a projectile. Included in their arsenal were rocks as big as cannonballs, stones for improvised slings, and spears made from sharpened sticks hardened in the fire.

Crabs, cooked in their own shells, proved to be a filling and delicious meal which renewed their strength. Afterwards, they washed down their meal with coconut milk. Then after quenching their thirst, the three castaways sat in silence contemplating their fate and wondering whether or not if this would be their last meal.

Johnny broke the silence by speaking wistfully of all the women that he had loved in the past and those destined never to be loved. This tragedy was not shared by young Simms who had never tasted the fruits of passion. Campbell, on the other hand, had no thoughts of love; loves lost, or love never to be had. His thoughts were terrible and dark. In his tortured imagination he began to recall stories passed on from sailor to sailor of the cannibals and the gruesome end of their captives, but the tale that he remembered vividly was the one told to him by Captain James Cook himself.

On his last voyage, Cook once again commanded HMS *Resolution*. Stewart Campbell served aboard as a cabin boy at the tender young age of 10. It was his second time on a ship, but this was a trip to be envied as it would secretly try to find the route of the Northwest Passage ... but it was mission that was destined end in disaster.

Campbell was delighted by the tales told by the officers as he served them at their dinner, but it was the Captain's stories that captured his imagination no matter how valiant or terrifying they could be. Captain Cook's vivid description of witnessing a human sacrifice now came flooding back into his memory.

*"I counted no less than forty- nine skulls" he began. "There upon an altar in the background they lay. There were sacrificed dogs and pigs on a scaffold and I waited for the feast to begin when the victim, a man bound and carried by two porters was brought in before the high chief Otoo. One of the presiding priests suddenly gouged out the left eye of the poor wretch who screamed in agony. The eye was put into the open mouth of the priest who then turned and presented to his Lord. This, they call "eating the man" or "food for the chief". Surely this is true as I observed traces of former times when other dead bodies had been feasted upon!"*

Cook, tragically, did not survive this last voyage. He was attacked by natives whom he had befriended in Hawaii when he had taken a chief hostage in order to regain a boat stolen by them. As Captain Cook turned his back to help launch the boats to escape, he was struck on the head by some villagers and then stabbed to death as he fell, face down in the surf. Hawaiian tradition says he was killed by a chief named Kalanimanokahoowaha. The Hawaiians then dragged his body away. Four marines were also killed, and two others were wounded in the confrontation. "The world lost a great man that day" Campbell lamented, "all because of a stupid boat!"

No one really slept that night though a cool, gentle breeze brought relief from the stifling heat of the day. In the darkness the dozing men imagined a plethora of dangers perceived by the snap of a twig by some prowling animal, or the sound of birds conversing amongst themselves. Could the birds be the cannibals readying for an attack? No one could be certain if the shadows that flitted about them were men, animals, or merely manifestations of their beleaguered minds.

Sunrise came early the next morning and so vanished the fears of phantasmal beings that exist only in the darkness. Daylight brought with it the hopes and dread that reality would bring as well. It wasn't a question of "if" but rather, "when" their enemy would appear. As predicted, they wouldn't have to wait very long.

Midshipman Simms was keeping watch from a promontory on the northernmost point of the Island. Two large war canoes, each about 30 ft. in length, were paddled by the most fearsome of savages and approaching rapidly. The largest of the men, whose face was tattooed in a most monstrous design, stood on scaffolding which connected the canoe to an outrigged float. Using his newly acquired skills in tree climbing, he shimmied up one of the palm trees designated as a warning tower. He gave the call "Caw, Caw, Caw", an indication of danger. The other men then scrambled back to meet Simms at their readied positions.

The rhythmic sound of a drum could be heard as the party drew nearer in their boat. As the massive canoe came closer to the shore; the men jumped into the surf and began to pull it onto the beach. Each of the castaways gathered a few spears and placed them within reach. There they stood; three against thirty. The odds were against them but surrender was never an option.

Then, a strange and curious event took place. As the Fijians (Campbell recognized this by their unique tattoos) approached, they stopped, turned to the largest and most fearsome looking of the bunch and started to laugh in low tones at first and then they burst out into full blown gales of laughter. Simms and Campbell were dumbstruck, but Johnny Burke's Irish temper got the best of him and he raised his spear, ready to strike.

"No, no, no, me friend…no!" shouted the giant Fijian. "We mean you no bad, we friend."

"Till you intend to eat us?" Johnny shouted.

"Mr. Burke, for heaven's sake, come to your senses!" Campbell shouted. "If they were going to attack us they would have done it by now!" The Bo'sun relented, much to the relief of his fellows, and within minutes the giant fellow and the castaways were talking.

"Our man fish and tell us he find the whitey men on Island. We think you get shipwreck in storm. We come, we rescue, you come back wid us. You stay here, you die. We good Christian, but mebbe de others not Christian." He explained in Pidgin English that his village had been converted by missionaries from New England. His people had welcomed the new religion and rejected the old one and its evil ways.

"Old priests be bad men. They kill and eat many our people too. We like new religion. People good and bring wid 'em good medicine too." He said that his name was Nah-ki-tee-roo which Campbell to his credit repeated until he pronounced the name correctly. The other men could only manage Naroo, which the big friendly native said was "okie by him".

"The tide will be in soon", Naroo warned. "We go now, catch wind home." He raised the canvas, took Campbell and Simms in his canoe and set a nervous Johnny Burke in the other. They arrived late in the afternoon and were welcomed by a small delegation of protestant missionaries and converted natives. Surely God, they reasoned, had kept them under his protection.

The Reverend and Mrs. Putnam were persons of the most admirable traits. Their unquestionable faith in God led them to leave a comfortable existence in their little New England town to bring his message of hope and salvation to the savages who inhabited the Islands of the South Pacific. It was not without great risk, as they did not enjoy the protection of a military presence, yet they struggled on with a gentle demeanor determined to bring the modern world with all the benefits of western medicine and sanitation, which was often lacking even in many parts of their own country.

The people who lived in these Islands did not live the happy existence recounted by sailors who invented tales of an idyllic paradise. There was warfare, there was sickness, and the oppression brought on by the priests who retained their power through taboos, human sacrifice, and cannibalism.

After passing the better part of a week under their care, Mr. Campbell began to question his hosts almost to the point of interrogation in regards to the natives' beliefs and customs. But it was of their religious beliefs that he had been most interested in, from their concept of creation and the reasons for human sacrifice. Of course, the inevitable question would arise: "Is cannibalism still practiced?"

The silence which ensued seemed to go on for an indeterminable length. It was clear that even the mention of the topic had stirred up memories of the Putnam's past trials that haunted them still. The couple looked at one another as if sharing a secret of unspeakable horror. Mrs. Putnam opened her mouth to speak but could only emit a gasping sound that was almost inaudible. Her husband put his hand upon hers which seemed to soothe her nerves before requesting if she could leave the two men to talk in private."

"Mr. Campbell … as you can imagine, our path was fraught with trials. It was no mean feat to bring the world of light to one so dark with sadness and unspeakable horror. We have been rewarded with much success, but we have also shared the misery inflicted upon us by a jealous king and his most evil servant, the high priest. As you can see, Mrs. Putnam and I are the only survivors of the original twelve missionaries still here who can bear witness to the unspeakable atrocities."

"I am so sorry for my ignorance Reverend. Sometimes I forget my manners when pursuing my curiosity."

"There is no reason for an apology Mr. Campbell. We live with many memories, some good and some bad. We cherish the memories of our most loved friends to be sure, but the memory of witnessing their sacrifice and the great heartache we suffered in burying their remains of what was left of them … mangled gnawed bones."

They called themselves "The Apostles", being twelve in the little group of missionaries. Besides the Putnams, there were three other married couples, two unmarried men, one widow, and a young woman barely in her late teens. Filled with the fervor of Evangelism in their breasts, all were committed to spreading the "Good News" of the Gospels. This they would do, even at the cost of their comfort or even sacrificing their own lives if God in his infinite wisdom decided martyrdom for them. It was duly noted that one of the unmarried men, a queer man whose faith bordered on fanaticism, had declared that he would welcome it.

They arrived on the big Island of Hawaii, where they received instruction from their predecessors on dealing with the people that they would minister to. The trip around Cape Horn through the Magellan Straits had been mercifully mild, according to the Captain of the *George F. Hunt*, but the "Apostles" suffered terribly from bouts of seasickness that plagued them since their departure. It is a fact that New England is noted for its fine ships and fearless seamen, but these goodly men and women were the sons and daughters of a more genteel class of merchants and farmers.

They found their places among the cargo in every little nook and cranny of the ship. Passengers were deemed less valuable than the merchandise stowed below deck. Seldom did the Apostles venture upon the deck as the "landlubbers", as they were referred to by the crew, always seemed to get themselves in the way of the sailors who scurried about the deck performing their duties under a harsh taskmaster.

Still, they endured every possible insult by man or by weather. There were rough seas and storms that blew in from nowhere it seemed to them. They prayed, sang hymns, and slept with the meager possessions that they had brought with them. It would all be worth it in the end, they hoped. The stories that they had been told of the Pacific Islands filled their imaginations with visions of a Garden of Eden with its perfect climate, lush greenery, abundance of food, and clear, clean water.

What the "Apostles" had expected to find and the reality that they discovered when they finally reached their Island Mission, south and west of Hawaii, was completely and utterly disheartening. Instead of finding a Utopian world of happy natives living in neat, kept huts with plenty of food and eager to hear the word of God, they found poor, emaciated savages living in squalor and eyeing them with bitter resentment. They were absolutely filthy and naked which upset the sensibilities of the younger women in their group. The huts which had been the homes of former missionaries who were either dead or had departed were teeming with every type of vermin whether it be mammalian, reptilian, or insect.

The Islanders were in a wretched state to be sure. These "well-formed" and "noble savages" described by Captain Cook had been decimated within the fifty odd years of contact with sailors from every "civilized" nation. With their insatiable lust for tropical beauties who felt no shame in lovemaking they brought a host of diseases, most notably smallpox, to a population having no immunity from them.

The Apostles bore their burdens as he who bore the cross for their own redemption. Hygiene was determined to be the first task to be undertaken. Any attempt to save their souls would have to wait while the most mortal cares were addressed. It was the women who took the lead in teaching the natives how to care for the most vulnerable of them, their children. They were horrified by the practice of infanticide, which was quite common, and the Apostles forbade the women to lay down with their brothers lest they give birth to the most pitiful and monstrous offspring.

Reverend Putnam and the other men did their best to instruct the men of the Island to clear the land in order to raise crops which they knew to be suitable for that climate. Putnam himself had been raised on a farm and was well suited for this duty. It was not easy to convince them though as the men were hunters and fishermen and it was the women and children who gathered the available fruits. They saw no need to work for so little gain.

The buildings, however, raised by the men of the missions fascinated the Islanders. They built strong framed houses of mud, wood, and thatch. It was not long before all were engaged in many building projects which culminated in the largest central structure of their community – the Church.

In actuality, it was more of a chapel than a church. Of course, it was windowless which allowed the cool breezes to blow through, while the roof was expertly thatched with palm leaves that gave protection from the blazing sun and deluges of rain that came without warning. Reverend Putnam created a vocabulary from the Islanders language as best he could by using English letters in combinations that replicated the sounds as closely as possible. Then, armed with newly devised methods of teaching, the "Apostles" were able to finally bring forth the Bible's truths, and with it, the hope for redemption.

There was baptism for those who professed a belief in their new religion. Children were taught to read the magic symbols on slates, and learned to make them "speak" as well using pieces of chalk. The good works and exemplary lives of the Apostles were highly esteemed by the populace they served, yet there were those in power who cast a malevolent eye on them and waited for their chance to pounce. Unbeknownst to them, the Islanders feared their king, the tyrannical Oh-too- hei and his treacherous priest, Kal-tu-ah!

## Attacked!

Reverend Putnam described the following events which changed the circumstances of the Apostle's Mission: "We, Mr. Poole and I, were returning to the Mission after spending the day evangelizing to the savages. The day was beautiful and fruitful. We baptized no less than 20 persons. I was quite pleased with the young man's comportment, he being very strong in his beliefs and sometimes too careless in word and actions. We were in the difficult position of winning the hearts and minds of the people. They were not to be persuaded to accept God's love with a sermon full of fire and brimstone so popular with many preachers in America. Many were convinced by Mr. Poole that by faith alone the penitant gave adoration to the true God, and that the grace bestowed upon them would conquer those that they feared. With those words many came to the water's edge and were baptized. Mr. Poole assured them that all their sins of the past would be washed away with the tide."

"And so, we rejoiced and expected to be greeted by our loved ones on our return- only to find the beaches empty. The silence was unnerving and we were uneasy when we found the Church and surrounding huts empty. To our horror we discovered the mangled and mutilated bodies of men, women, and children. They were slaughtered where they stood and lay in heaps one on top of one another." I searched for my wife and companions. We found only the men, but not one of our women." Reverend Putnam paused a moment. Tears welled up in his eyes. The memories of that day haunted him still as if it happened only yesterday.

It was uncharacteristic for Mr. Campbell to sit patiently while the Reverend collected himself. He hung his head in silence and wrung his hands while reliving the memory of that day. He steadied himself and then asked: "Could you be so kind to tell me where I left off?" Campbell thought it odd but obliged him.

"You were telling me about the day you found the Mission in disarray…"

"Disarray? They were slaughtered! And it was clear to us that it was the King who ordered it. Upon a slate, one of the children wrote the name of that murderous beast – King!"

The Reverend had no time to bury the dead as Mr. Poole had requested. They arranged the bodies as best they could with the hope that they could give them a decent burial … when – or if, they returned.

Reverend Putnam and Mr. Poole took water and some food with them as they made their way back to their canoe. They paddled their way out to sea and headed to the Island known to the natives as "Taboo". It was there that King Oh-too- hei and his priest, Kal-tu-ah conducted their ghastly sacrifices. With fire in their breasts the two men paddled with the strength and vigor of ten as they were desperate to save the women from a most hideous and cruel fate that surely awaited them.

The Island, silhouetted by the sun setting on the horizon, was within their reach. Putnam and Poole made their way to the shore slowly and carefully, fearing they might tear their outrigger on the coral reef. A dreadful noise was heard in the distance which struck fear into the men. Was that the sound of the victim they heard? Surely they must not fail. Evil cannot, and must not prevail!

Landfall was made in complete darkness. Fearing that their canoe would be discovered, they pulled it far from the beach and hid it beneath some bushes. Unaided by the light of Sun or Moon, the men grasped and clawed their way through the rotted wood and wetland while swarms of insects bit them incessantly. They were drawn to flicker of light that grew and grew upon their approach. Another deafening scream led them closer to its source. It was a man screaming and yelling in a savage tongue. Then … a blood curdling shriek - this time it was a woman!

"Mr. Poole, to his credit, never wavered though I still bear the shame of being struck with a terror that held me to my spot as if I were petrified as was Lot's wife! He shook me to my senses and led me to the edge of a clearing where the most gruesome event was taking place."

"Two of our women had been stripped naked and were being roasted alive while the savages, men, women, and children alike, howled like wild animals awaiting their feast. A third was held down on a stone by a group of men as their priest, Kal-tu-ah, a giant of a man strode over to the screaming woman, gouged out her left eye and held it in his teeth. He looked 'round to find King Oh-too- hei smacking his lips. The King then plucked the eye from the Priest's mouth, and chewed it with relish."

Putnam and Poole held their tongues as the woman was mercifully dispatched with a blow of a club. "Where were the others?" they wondered. The area was searched with much difficulty as the only light they had was that of the flickering sacrificial fire. Finally they came upon a group of small huts that lay in a circle around the King's house where they found Mrs. Putnam, the Widow Smith, and young Esther Kane. The women were joyous for their rescue, but still feared pursuit by the natives who were in a state of frenzy stirred by the high priest's rituals.

The five remaining Apostles made their way back toward the boat. scratched by tree branches, cut by saw grass, and constantly being assaulted by swarms of vicious parasites of every variety. The canoe was just within reach when all of a sudden they were spotted by one of the savages patrolling the beach. He let out such a loud scream that the drums stopped beating instantly and wild war hoops filled the dark sky.

The men hurried the women into the boat and pushed them out as far as they could go. "Row, row, for your lives!" they shouted. The natives crowded the beach and a group of warriors swam out in an effort to secure the boat. Putnam and Poole, realizing that the savages would soon reach them, were pulled into the boat and paddled furiously to escape their tormentors. Esther Kane screamed as hands reached over the side in an attempt to take the canoe. They who had tried to save souls now were caught in a struggle to save their own lives. The Reverend, a peaceable man was at first reluctant to strike a blow, but Mr. Poole with a righteous anger brought down his paddle hard upon their attackers heads, splitting them and spilling their blood into the black water. One by one the numbers decreased until the men's energies were exhausted.

Just when they thought all were dead and they were safe, a bloodied hand reached round and pulled young Esther to the edge of the boat. She let out a blood curdling scream that brought about a gale of laughter from the savages on the beach. Widow Smith, good woman that she was, responded in an instant. A big, strong woman used to a lifetime of hard labor, grabbed the man by his hair and pounded his head repeatedly on the side of the boat. The hands slipped away, as did the savage, into the sea. "Food for the devil fish!" she exclaimed while wiping her bloody hands on her dress.

Mr. Campbell sat in amazement as the Reverend finished his tale. Despite their trials and multiple scrapes with the King, the people turned away from him and came to accept God's good news of redemption.

"The Widow, now in her eighties, survives still. Mr. Poole and Ms. Kane were married, raised a family and till this day continue their mission…"

Campbell, who realized that Captain Cook's account had been proven true, begged to know what became of the King and the Priest.

"The King died. He caught a disease from one of the woman whom he lusted for…syphilis, I believe. He lived several years but had completely lost his mind. He ended his days confused and with the mind of a young child - cared for by the very missionaries he had once vowed to kill"

"And… of the priest?" Campbell urged.

"No one has ever seen him. No one returns to the Island as far as can be known. Naroo tells me that the natives said that he was killed by the spirits of those he killed…"

"Surely you don't believe it Reverend?"

"But, I do Mr. Campbell. God's vengeance was upon him. As for myself I could not prove the tale's veracity as none will venture near the Island. There is not a soul there to be saved, and so, my work and I … remain here."

Mr. Campbell's thirst for answers would not be quenched. That evening, he and Johnny Burke sat by a fire under a starlit sky and spoke in subdued tones. Young Mr. Simms, who had discovered his first love in the form of a beautiful native girl, had been absent for some time. His desire to return to duty now seemed so distant and far away. The young girl, who was studying to be a missionary, would also be tested in her vocation.

Campbell and Burke were resigned to life at sea. It was all that they had ever known. Love was a game for the handsome and brawny boatswain, and if he ever knew it at all, Angus Campbell considered it as nothing but a nuisance for a man at his age.

"It won't be long Johnny that we two will be back aboard ship eating, sleeping, and living in filth. Let us enjoy our freedom while it lasts."

Johnny Burke stretched his muscled arms behind his head and lay back with his eyes on the stars above him. He sighed, and grumbled: "If the ship never returned … it would be quite fine by meself." Burke had been lured into the Island lifestyle and being a man well acquainted with boats he dreamed of a life far from the rigors of life aboard a ship and the demands of a tyrannical captain.

"Yes Johnny", Campbell went on. "Tis a shame to waste one's life when opportunity can be found all around us... and that Island that they call Taboo. I am sure that riches can be had there, but alas, there is no one brave enough to gather the spoils."

Campbell hoped that the seed was planted in Johnny's brain. "Who would be the wiser if we never returned from Taboo Island? Surely we could say that it was an extremely dangerous mission, in the interest of Science, of course. The natives feared going there, but only they knew the way. Naroo could show them the way. They would gather anything valuable, then, they would escape to a life of leisure and most importantly, freedom!

Like a hungry fish Johnny took the bait – hook, line and sinker! The two decided to keep the secret between them. Even poor young Mr. Simms, if they could even find him, would never know of the plans they hatched that night. "It's for his own welfare" quipped Burke.

In order to travel to the Island which they knew to be within a day's journey the two men sought out information from Naroo, the fierce looking Native who had rescued them from their island prison.

Naroo had just returned from fishing and all enjoyed a hearty meal as it was the custom of the natives to share alike.

After eating and drinking their fill, the two men drew their pipes out for a smoke. Naroo looked at them curiously as gray puffs of smoke exited their mouths and noses. Johnny Burke entertained the little ones by blowing smoke rings into the air that dissolved into nothingness unless interrupted by the nimble hands attempting to catch them. They shared the aromatic tobacco with their new friend who drew in a great breath of smoke only to blow it out in a coughing fit. Naroo decided that it was only good for white men.

Then the subject came up about visiting the Island of Taboo where the three women of the Apostles met their grisly deaths. Naroo decidedly was against any trip to that dark and dreary place filled with the spirits of the dead, but most of all he feared the living corpse of the High Priest. It was said that he sat amongst the bones of his victims, his mouth full of a precious pearl as big as an eye. "No one go there no more! Putnam say we stay away, it place of Devils."

"Surely you don't believe that he is still alive?" Campbell laughed.

"He dead, but he still roam 'round the place."

"Well if he is, then he'll get a bit of this!" Johnny cried, shaking his giant fist.

"Naroo don't go. You no go either. Taboo bad, Taboo evil, no God on Taboo."

"Well we don't know the direction. There are many Islands out there. How would you find your way? There's no map for us anyway" Campbell sighed.

It was then that Naroo quietly pulled a little net of knotted string that resembled a spider's web from the little pouch he kept tied around his waist. He took the web and held it up for them to see. The knot in the center of the web he told them was the Island that they were on. From the center, there were strings radiating from their island knot to other knots tied on the strings, some longer and some shorter. The shorter knots, he told them were of one day's journey, twice the length, two days, and so on. The Direction was determined by the Sun from east to west and so, north and south were perpendicular.

"Johnny, I believe that he is showing us a map of his people's design. So this is the way they navigated all these years!"

Campbell was determined to get the direction from Naroo who was unwilling to tell them. It was surely one of the closest knots, but in which direction? The best way to loosen the tongue of this giant would be gotten by one of the oldest tricks ever devised – they would get Naroo drunk!

The Hawaiian natives derived from the ti plant a fermented beverage that they called Okolehao. It was commonly referred to as the native's "beer". With the introduction of the Englishmen's method of distillation, it became a potent alcoholic drink. Campbell secured it from some of the natives and decided to use it on the unsuspecting Naroo.

Within twenty minutes or so the drink had produced the desired effect. Naroo was laughing and teasing them with his little spider's web declaring "Naroo know, but he no tells you!" He was, however, eventually tricked into divulging the right knot. Campbell and Burke had been prepared with provisions to leave at any time. So at sunrise the next morning, they headed South and East toward the Island of Taboo

## Taboo

Campbell and Johnny were delighted to find that the journey was actually shorter than the day's journey that they anticipated. It was approximately two or three in the afternoon and the sun shone bright on the glimmering sea. A large flying fish jumped up out from the waves and into the boat which the men regarded it as a welcoming sign. The little sail was dropped and then too, their paddles. They rejoiced in finding a sandy bottom and easily walked onto the beach with their craft pulled behind.

"Well Johnny" Campbell chuckled, "this is the beginning of the rest of an easy life for us. Let the fools break their backs. I tell you lad, there's riches to be found on this 'ere place!"

Johnny chortled in agreement but noticed the thick bushes not far from the pristine beach. "I say mate, how do we even get into the place?"

The paunchy Campbell looked at Johnny for a moment, walked over to the boat and brandished two short swords he had bought as souvenirs some time ago. "We'll just slash our way through, me boy-oh!"

The men decided to sup with the flying fish and then make a fresh start the next morning. The Sun greeted them as they lay next to the remains of last night's campfire. Both men went giddily to their work but alas found it much more difficult than they could have imagined. Johnny' broad strokes felled much of the brush and small trees, but Campbell, being unfamiliar with hard, physical labor, chopped here and there following Johnny as a shark would a ship's wake in search of an easy meal.

It was indeed a dark and dreary place that they travelled through. The rocks were covered with moss and the ground was often saturated. The men suffered from the merciless biting insects and felt surrounded by unknown terrors slithering beneath them or hanging above. Johnny had begun to doubt his decision, yet Angus Campbell was determined to find his "El Dorado".

Just as they were about to give up for the day and return to the beach, Mr. Campbell spotted large stone carved figures called "Tiki" by the savages. These fearsome sculptures represented their warlike

gods. He hastened toward it, and from that position, spotted another, then in the distance – another. "Johnny, I believe we have come upon the road to our destiny. These stones will lead us to the village. I have heard that there are many precious items and stones to be found there. Some say that there are pearls as big as ostrich eggs as well – and all for the picking! Not one of those superstitious fools would dare come here, but we are Englishmen and afraid of nothing!"

Johnny chafed somewhat under his boasts. He had never liked Mr. Campbell before. He was lazy, curried favor with the Captain, and now wanted to become his bosom friend. His trust was waning. After all, Campbell knew little more than he did that the stories he was told were true. Suppose he had been lied to, or even worse, made to be a fool?

"Eureka, I've found it! Campbell shouted. Looking like a madman he jumped up and down shaking his fat body like a bowl of jelly. Then, with a burst of uncharacteristic energy, he cleared the vines off which revealed a large, oblong slab. "It's the sacrificial altar Johnny … ye can yet see the bloodstains on it!"

He shuddered for moment thinking about the awful scenes that had taken place here. "That man is absolutely daft" he thought as he recoiled at the sight of the stained rock. It would take forever to clear the rest of the area. Would it be worth their trouble?

"I see the remains of some huts between those trees yonder. An' I'll be surprised if the big one didn't belong to the King … that's where the treasure is Johnny. We just have to cut our way to it!"

For the first time in his life Angus Campbell slashed with the effort of three men. He cut a path toward the largest of the dilapidated houses; he cleared the steps and then bounded through the door.

Suddenly, Johnny heard a scream of horror from Mr. Campbell. He hurried toward the house and found a nightmarish scene. The mummified body of Kal-tu-ah was seated upon the throne of the

King, adorned in beautiful feathers with a terrible and terrifying look upon its face. Lying in front of the macabre figure lay the body of Angus Campbell with his right hand clutching his chest.

Johnny figured correctly that Campbell's exertion after a lifetime of soft living had caused his heart to stop beating. "Damned fool!" he said to himself. "And what now of his "treasure" … For what shall it profits a man, if he shall gain the whole world, and lose his own soul?"

There was eeriness about the place that struck fear into the sailor. He decided to gather what he could, leaving Campbell's body where it lay, and make his way back to the boat. There was a quick search for precious stones and gold but none were to be found. Johnny looked up at the mummy and decided that its sardonic grin was too much for him to bear, so with a whack of his sword he took off the head of the high priest. As it fell to the ground Johnny saw something white and lustrous peep out from the mouth of the decapitated head.

"Could it be?" he wondered, "the egg-sized pearl of which the natives had spoken?" He looked closer assured himself that indeed it was the pearl. "I'll be takin' that for me troubles priest!" he laughed. He tried to open the mouth to extract the pearl but only succeeded in getting it halfway. Time after time he tried pushing aside the lips but they seemed to snap back in place.

"I'll be having this if it be the last thing that I do" he screamed. With one hand he grabbed the hideous thing, tucked it under his arm, and with his other hand pried the jaw until it was almost free. Suddenly he felt the thing squirm under his arm and its jaws came down on his fingers with a vise-like grip. Johnny became terrified as he struggled to remove his fingers from the mummy's mouth. He managed to get his fingers out from the mouth when the top digit of his little finger was bitten off by the snapping jaws! A profusion of blood gushed forth from his hand as he flung the head into a dark corner. Flying insects started to swarm in the room and Johnny ran for his life.

Johnny was pursued by these winged demons but found that the cleared path gave him an easy access to the beach – sanctuary from the bloodsucking mosquitos. With a mighty leap he flew into the boat and paddled like a madman out to the deep water. Day turned to night and night to day. He was hopelessly lost and dreaded dying of thirst surrounded by water that he should not, could not drink.

The Sun beat down on his bared head and he thought he had died when he could see the long haired silhouetted figure of a man which he perceived to be the Christ bend down to pluck him from the boat. "Take me into thy hand's oh lord" he muttered in his delirium.

"It not be time yet for you Johnny" the figure laughed. The voice was familiar, but he could not recognize it. After a few draughts of fresh water revived him, he sat in the boat face to face with the man who had saved him. It was Naroo! Johnny thanked him, God, and anyone that he could think of as his life had been spared.

"And so," the Boatswain said as he was finishing his story, "the thing you hold precious is within." The crowd clapped and cheered. Mr. Cherry asked who would be the next to tell a story and looked about the room. It was during that time that I thought it most advantageous for me to ask this young actor if he would be available in the future for one of the costumed galas given by the Wanamaker family this spring.

"I say – that was a most enjoyable tale. Your acting was impeccable as well. Would you be interested in telling some stories at an event? You will be well paid.

"Well, Mr. Sportin' Jack, I am very much obliged but I tell my story but for this group alone" he said as he put on his broad brimmed straw hat. My story is true, you see, and there's only one reason to tell it."

"And that is?" I asked.

"So that the unbelievers will believe" he said with a smile.

I asked him by what name I should call him as I went to shake his hand goodbye.

"That would be Johnny … Johnny Burke."

"Come now!" I chortled. As I reached out my hand to shake his, he deferred to his own. I took notice of that muscled hand to discover a missing digit on the little finger! My eyes focused on the stubby finger as he disappeared into the crowd.

As I turned around I noticed that Mr. Cherry had a broad grin on his face and a twinkle in his eye. Was I the butt of a practical joke or could I have really been talking to a ghost?

## <u>Chapter 5 - The Tale of the Zampognaro</u>

The lightheartedness returned and once again the air was filled a cacophony of diverse languages filling the room. Some were recognizable; the rapid-fire staccato of a Spaniard, the guttural utterings of a Frenchman, and the distinctive cockney, but there were also those of which I had not a clue of the origin. It was then a familiar voice – that of Mr. Cherry, who seemed to be a little agitated that the proceedings were being interrupted for much too long as the clock drew nearer to midnight - the witching hour!

"Shall we have another story?" he bellowed while whipping 'round in his cape and almost losing his ridiculously tall stovepipe hat with the maneuver. "Must I remind you that our time is growing short? Who of you will tell their story?"

There was a silence, followed by whispers, and a flurry of movement about in the room. I saw an Egyptian princess speaking with a medieval knight. The two, despite speaking different languages, went on as if no language barrier existed – it was very strange to me that they seemed to understand each other perfectly.

Just then when it seemed that no one could make up their minds to step forth, the piercing sound of a bagpiper tuning his instrument filled the air with one long and lingering note.

"I will tell my story!" said the bagpiper with a distinctive Italian accent. Having made the acquaintances of many Italians from South "Philly", the sound of the bagpipes, or zampogna, was not new to me. Though I detested the sounds of bagpipes, Irish, Scottish, or Italian (take your pick), the mechanics of that instrument combined with a sheep or goat bladder to harness the air which was then forced through the pipes produced an impressive volume.

Into the light given off by the fire at the hearth stepped a little dark man dwarfed by his instrument. The costume was a traditional one that must have predated our current time by at least a century. His small round head was covered by a black, red tasseled stocking cap that reached past his shoulder and hung on his right shoulder. A tunic, also black, was beautifully embroidered in red, green, and white like the Italian flag. Brass buttons ran down the front of his vest and a white blouse peeked through at the throat and wrists. His trousers were black as well and stopped at a pair of the most exquisite pair of shoes that resembled Turkish slippers. He could have passed for a Turk as well with his dark eyes and bushy black moustache that concealed his mouth when he wasn't speaking. His nose, long and thin, ran down to that great moustache and gave it the appearance of a push broom!

"Good Evening Signore and Signori" He began. "Tonight I will tell you a true story … or, at least they say it is true, in a little village where I played my Zampogna some time ago. It is a story of an ugly man, a handsome man, a beautiful girl, and a horrible witch, or as we say in Italian… a Strega! This story, I will tell as I have heard it. You can believe it or not Mr. Sportin' Jack … see if I care … but listen carefully!"

Many, many years ago there was another Zampognaro named Rodolpho. As a boy, he grew up on a farm in Abruzzo which was located high, way up high, in the mountains. In fact it was so high that they called the nearest town L'Aquila, or "The Eagle"! The land was as poor as the people and young Rodolpho yearned for a life of adventure, fame and fortune. But to his misfortune he was an ugly child with coarse red hair, big ears and long lanky limbs like your President Lincoln. The children of the village teased him so much that he decided that he would find his fame and fortune at sea, and so, he left the mountain village and travelled to Pescara, a fishing town on the Adriatic coast.

But dear people, there was no adventure to be found there either. The work was hard and Rodolpho was no fisherman. He spent days on end repairing the great nets used to catch the fish. He was bored, lonely and taunted by the people for his looks. Yet the boy, almost a man now, became strong, careful with his money, and virtuous. He was determined to return to L'Aquila and with his money he would become a shepherd so that he could live his life far away from the mean taunts of the ignorant villagers.

When the young man had decided that he had saved enough money to return home, he bought some provisions, packed them in his sack, and set off for his journey. As he passed by the docks he heard a whimper. "It sounds like a dog" he thought to himself. Looking round, he saw nothing and decided to resume his journey ... then heard a faint bark. This time he was determined to find the animal. He tilted his head to the side, and with his large ear was able to trace the barking to a mound of old nets, discarded by the fishermen.

"Where are you little one?" he called out. The barking became stronger and stronger. Rodolpho looked frantically through the tangled rope and discovered a puppy hopelessly tangled in the web. He was dirty, cold and wet. The puppy's soulful eyes were large and black and touched Rodolpho's heart. The lad was as kind as he was ugly.

"I will take care of you my little one. We will become the best of friends and we will never be lonely again." So he cleaned the puppy, fed it, and put him in his sack. Then the two companions left Pescara for good and never looked back.

Did I tell you what Rodolpho had named the dog? I must have forgotten. Well, as he found him in the fisherman's net he called him "Netto", which is Italian - for net!

The life of a shepherd, as you may have guessed, can be a lonely one. There can be many days (sometimes weeks) that he spends his time all alone watching his flock grazing up on the hillside. So to occupy himself he plays a pipe or a stringed instrument, but the prized possession of the lonely shepherd is a Zampogna. Yes, I know it is an odd looking instrument and it can take some time to learn how to play it, but there is no other instrument quite as wonderful as the Zampogna!

When one is up in the mountains you can hear the beautiful notes playing like an angel singing. The sheep gather around while the shepherd lulls them to sleep with his tunes. Of course, it takes some time to learn to play the zampogna to make it sound beautiful, but when the shepherd learns, then, it is like magic! Well, let me get back to my story…

As you may know, the nights are very cold in the mountains. Sometimes the Shepherd makes a shelter, and sometimes he finds a cave to shelter for the night (there are many caves in the Apennine Mountains). Well, one night, Rodolpho and his dog Netto, who, unfortunately, was as ugly as his master, were sheltering in a cave when a snow storm came down unexpectedly in a fury; I believe that you call it a "Blizzard". He quickly built a roaring fire after hurrying his sheep out of the dangerous weather and inside of the cave. Netto, as it turned out, was an excellent sheepdog, though what breed (or breeds as he was surely a mongrel) was uncertain.

"Alas my dear Netto, we are safe and warm in this cave. My heart is sad for anyone or anything caught outside tonight. Netto nuzzled his ugly little face against Rodolpho's thigh, while his master took a deep breath and blew into the bladder of the Zampogna.

The shrill sound of tuning the pipes would have startled any other dog, but Netto was not only an ugly dog, but he was deaf as well. His ears, as large as they were, heard nothing … a cruel joke of nature … wouldn't you agree?

Rodolpho played his pipes sweetly while he watched his sheep settling down for the night. His playing always seemed to lull them into a slumber each night. After he had played for the better part of an hour, he too started to feel the weight of Hypnos's fingers tugging at his eyelids. Just as he was putting his Zampogna to rest he thought he heard the sound of wailing. "Surely it must be some poor beast" he thought to himself. Then he heard it again. This time the sound was closer and more distinct. It was the sound of a human cry!

"Netto my friend, someone is out in that awful storm. I must go and find them. Stay here and guard my sheep." Netto, being deaf, could only see his master's lips moving, but he immediately understood the command when Rodolpho's made the motion to "stay" with his hand.

Rodolpho sighed and hated the thought of going out into that awful weather, but he was determined to do his best to retrieve the poor soul stranded on the rocky landscape surrounding the cave. He yelled out "Hullooooo! Can you hear me?" He called out several times and heard nothing. His heart raced. Was he too late to save the person? He called out over and over again, and just when he thought that all was lost, he heard the plaintive weeping of a woman huddled between the spaces in the rocks behind him.

"Don't worry! I am here. I will save you!"

There was no response from the limp figure. Rodolpho, with his strong arms pulled her up and cradled her to his chest as a mother would do with a babe. He threw his sheepskin cloak over her, and fought his way through the bitter cold and driving sleet back to the cave. Though it was a short journey to safety, each step he took was fraught with danger. One unfortunate step would hurtle them downward into an abyss of white death.

The cruel wind showed no pity pushing the rescuer ever closer to the edge of a precipice. It whistled and screamed as if mocking him, yet Rodolpho, nimble as a mountain goat, reached the cave safe and sound. Netto sensed his master's return and rose from his slumber to greet him with the strange bundle he laid upon the floor of the cave. He sniffed and sniffed until his master shooed him away. "Stay away boy!" Rodolpho hissed. Netto sensed the anger quickly dissolve into regret as his master's hand now petted him on his head lovingly.

"Netto, it seems we have a guest for the evening and I do believe that she will be alright." The light from the fire revealed something unexpected. There, laying in front of him in a deep slumber was the most beautiful woman that he had ever laid his eyes upon. Her hair was a fiery red, her large eyes were framed by long lashes, and the whitest skin was tinted with the slightest blush upon the cheeks. Her brow was wide, the nose - exquisite with a slight turning up at the tip, and the most beautiful full red lips… redder than any rose.

His heart ached like never before. He had never known love and knew that this beautiful woman would find him to be repulsive as did all the others. He looked at his ugly dog and sighed: "It is good that we have each other as none would have us." Netto cocked his head as if straining to listen, but he would hear nothing with his deaf ears.

## Rodolpho in Love

Rodolpho spent every waking moment caring for the beautiful young woman. Her breathing became stronger and although he gave thanks to the Lord above for her recovery, the poor shepherd's heart was breaking. She would not wake unto a handsome prince, but rather, an ugly man unworthy of her love.

"Sleep, my love, and let me behold thy beauty for a little while longer" he sighed. Netto lay besides her keeping her warm with his body and the three spent the night safe and warm by the fire as the storm raged outside in all its fury.

Rodolpho rose early as was his custom, and began to feed his flock … little that he had. "It is a good thing that the storm has ceased to blow as I have nothing to give them to eat" he said petting Netto's fuzzy brow. Suddenly, he saw something that made him rejoice and recoil at the same time. The woman reached over and began to pet the dog. She opened her eyes slowly and fearful that she might be afraid upon beholding his ugliness, the shepherd turned his head from the light and said: "I worried that you would never wake" he lied, "but it is through God's grace that you are alive and well!"

"My dear sir" she replied. "I remember gathering flowers on the mountain side for my sick mother when I was beset by a terrible storm. I took shelter among the rocks but believed that I would die a wretched death unsheltered from the cold. You have saved me. How can I ever repay you?"

Rodolpho, ever so humble, replied in his gentle manner that no recompense was needed but to regain her strength. She asked him his name, which he told her, and added that he was only a poor shepherd. "When I heard your cry whilst playing my pipes", Rodolpho explained, "It was merely my duty as a Christian to help anyone who was lost in the storm. Christ taught us that the Good Shepherd would search to find his lost sheep.

The young woman, her name was Rosa, begged him to come closer so that she could gaze upon him. He hesitated for a moment, gathered his courage, and then walked into the light, his head bowed down. Netto gleefully wagged his scruffy tale and rubbed against his master's thigh.

"Why do you hold your head down Rodolpho?"

"You are so beautiful Rosa, and I am ashamed of my ugliness" he stammered.

"I see no ugliness in you. Your heart is pure. Where there is such goodness there can be nothing that would keep me from loving you. Step into the light!"

"He did as she commanded. She beheld him as a love-struck maiden would. He could not believe his fortune. Surely he was dreaming!" Rosa held his hand and looked into his eyes. His heart swelled in his breast and his head felt as if he were about to faint. Rosa got up from where she lay, embraced him and kissed his lips.

Rodolpho was unable to understand what was happening to him. Every bone in his body seemed to shift within and his nose was no longer visible as he glanced from side to side.

"What has happened to my nose?" he thought. "Surely I can always see the tip from the corner of my eye?" He put his hands up to his face. He did not see the rough and bony hands of a shepherd, but fine, smooth hands like those of a gentleman. He quickly felt his face for his nose. It was there, of course, but was much smaller! He looked down to find Netto tugging at his sleeve, but to his joy he beheld a dog with soft and beautiful white fur. His eyes were black, as well as his little nose.

The dog licked at his hand. Rodolpho called for Netto, but he was nowhere to be found. "Surely this is not my dog" he thought.

He called again and the little white dog jumped up again.

"Rosa" he said, "My dog had gone and this dog has taken his place."

"I know of no other dog Rodolpho. It was he who lay by my side the entire night. What a fine dog you have! His eyes are bright and black as coal, his coat as soft as a lamb's."

Rodolpho was overjoyed. Surely a miracle had taken place! He quickly made the sign of the cross and then the two breakfasted on some bread and cheese. The storm had abated and soon the sun rays began to melt the snow. He had wished that they could stay in their happy little cave for a while longer but Rosa began to grow worried about her mother.

"Rodolpho, my mother is old and frail. I am sure that she is sick with worry for me. I must go to her at once."

But Rosa, you are much too weak to travel. I can go to tell her that you are fine and that I will take you home as soon as you are well enough to travel. I must get some food as well. You will be safe with Netto by your side."

And so the poor shepherd, unaware of his newly acquired beauty set off to visit Rosa's mother. Passing through the village, he noticed that the women all looked at him with desire rather than the disgust that he was accustomed to. He thought it strange but journeyed on to the little cottage which lay nearby. There he spied a pretty little house surrounded by flowers of every sort. "Why would Rosa go to pick flowers on the mountainside while the flowers were here in abundance?" He gave no other thought about it and walked to the door. He knocked, but no one answered. He called out but … no response. Just as he was about to turn away he was confronted by an ugly old crone who asked him his business there.

Although her looks were repulsive, Rodolpho remembered the pain he felt as others had turned away from him. He stood up, gathered his breath and blurted out: "I am here to see the mother of Rosa. She is well and I am taking good care of her until she is well enough to return.

"Oh happy day!" the woman responded. "I have been worried about my Rosa and thought I would never see her again!"

The woman seemed less ugly, Rodolpho thought to himself. "It was her sorrow that had distorted her face so."

Rodolpho spent some time recounting his story to the old woman, but remembered that he must return soon before sundown. The grateful mother plied him with victuals and offered what little money that she had, though the young man refused it.

'Please promise me that you will love and care for my daughter. I am sure that she has already fallen in love with you as you are so handsome and kind!"

Rodolpho chuckled to himself remembering her words as he made his way back to his mountain home. As the sun was strong, he began to thirst. He bent down along the side of a stream, cupped his hands, and before he could put them into the water was shocked to see an image of a handsome man with flaming red hair, trim mustache and dark eyes staring back at him!

"Surely I am dreaming." He blinked his eyes – the handsome man did the same. He twirled his moustache – again the same!

Rodolpho laughter thundered and echoed throughout the hills. "Praise God – a miracle!"

The poor shepherd ran as swift as a deer through hill and valley with his heart ready to burst. It was only now that he felt worthy of the love of the beautiful Rosa who met him at the mouth of the cave, her strength invigorated, and with a loving embrace.

"Oh Rosa, God has performed a miracle! No longer will I bear the insults of those who ridiculed me for my ugliness, now that I am handsome."

"Rodolpho, I knew only your heart. It was by your kindness that I came to fall in love with you. I love you and will stay by your side if you would'st take me as your wife and be forever faithful."

It was then that Rodolpho, his heart full of emotion, gave his pledge to marry Rosa and to be faithful until his dying day. Netto consented to the proposal by rubbing his head against his master's thigh.

Rosa took leave of Rodolpho on a fine spring morning. He promised to visit her often which he did many evenings when her mother was fast asleep. The two young lovers embraced under the moon and stars and made their plans to be together as man and wife.

"As soon as I can afford a proper house we shall wed. I am a poor shepherd, it is true, but I am earnest and diligent. Pray that our wish may come soon my dearest Rosa."

"It will be soon Rodolpho for I love you and know that good fortune will befall you." And with those last words spoken, they kissed and parted.

On the very next morning Rodolpho and Netto gathered the flock and made their way to the village to shear them and sell the wool for what he could. To his amazement, the wool was determined to be of the highest quality every to be had. Forgetful of his newly acquired looks, he was shocked that he was unknown to the people of the village who treated him with the most respect. The young women, much admiring of this handsome (and now prosperous) young shepherd, threw at him the most audacious glances. Such flirtations would have been normally considered by the mothers of these girls to be abominable, but now, as they considered him to be a very eligible husband, they ignored the impropriety.

Rodolpho had not been recognized, nor could he explain the circumstances that had befallen him. Thus he spoke to Netto, his oldest and dearest friend. "Netto if I am to be believed, would this transfiguration be considered grace from our Father in Heaven, or would it be considered the work of the Devil. Surely I am innocent of any misdeed, but consortium with Lucifer and his minions is punishable by death. It would be unwise to reveal myself!"

The poor man stroked Netto's fine white fur while he thought over his plight. Suddenly, he smiled and said: "My dear friend, it would not be impossible that I should have a cugino (cousin) who could be handsome. My hair, still the color of flame, my voice, never course, my language, never vulgar, I shall now be known as Roberto!"

And so Rodolpho was forever gone! From this point no one would know the deception … no one, except Rosa!

As Rodolpho's wealth increased, the attention paid to him by the pretty young women of the village did as well. Unaccustomed as he was to amorous temptations, he fell prey to lust and licentious behavior. His visits to his beloved Rosa became less frequent while his unfaithfulness became more frequent.

News spreads quickly in the small Italian towns that dot the mountains of Abruzzo. It was not long before word of the newcomer Roberto's engagement to the mayor's daughter, Ginevra, a beautiful girl with the bluest eyes and golden hair that hung to her slim waist fell upon the ears of the suspicious Rosa.

Rodolpho became occupied with the upcoming nuptials. He was feted by the town's wealthy patrones and the bans of marriage were announced in the church. During this time it became nearly impossible for Rodolpho to make his clandestine trips to Rosa, the woman he had pledged to marry and be faithful until his last breath.

"Surely my promise was made in the heat of passion" he reasoned. "Rosa is a beautiful girl and surely will marry and forget me." But though he tried to convince himself otherwise, it was on one of his occasional nocturnal visits that Rosa's suspicions of his infidelity aroused his feelings of guilt.

"Rodolpho, you have been away for so much time. My mother questions me daily of your intentions. Have you been faithful to me?"

Swallowing hard, he stammered: "never would I be untrue, but if thou have lost your feeling for me than you can set me free to love again!"

No man who was truly in love would say such a thing. Much to his dismay, Rosa embraced him kissed him on the lips and whispered "I will love you always and never leave you." Unable to resist her charms Rodolpho momentarily forgot his troubles and allowed "the old man in the moon" to witness their passion once again.

Rosa kissed him as he lay upon the meadow grass and then silently made her way home lest her mother discover her gone from the house. Rodolpho whistled for Netto and the two made their way back to the village and resumed his identity as his "cousin" once again.

The bands of matrimony were read for the third and last time in the village church between Ginevra Corsetti, and "Roberto Da Veneto", the cousin of Rodolpho D' Aquila. The Mayor was proud of his son-in-law to be and made a formal announcement that the marriage that would take place on the following Saturday and would be followed by a magnificent celebration opened to all in the village.

As you may well know, Italians, especially the rustics, celebrate for any reason, and therefore there are so many Saint's day festivities marking the calendar each year. The Mayor had been a wine merchant who owned the best vineyards in the area. Wine would flow like water and music, of course, would fill the air. The shrill pipes of the Zampogna signaled the call for those experts to dance to the delight of the onlookers. "Roberto", who had mentioned to the Mayor that he was fond of playing the Zampogna, was surprised to find a gift waiting for him as he returned to his lodgings.

"What could this present be Netto?" he wondered. Netto sniffed the package, which was quite large, then walked away dismissively as there was nothing which he would be interested in. "Ah, my little friend. There will be plenty of food. I assure you that you will eat well as I am marrying well and will not forget my dearest companion."

This present was something new for Rodolpho. As ugly as he had been, he had never been given a present in his whole life. An envelope was fastened to the package with the words: "To be opened on our Wedding day" written in a most exquisite script.

Rodolpho's head was filled with thoughts for his future and he had completely forgotten his pledge to marry Rosa. He had not seen her for quite some time and reasoned that she had forgotten him. As he lay in his bed with Netto at his side, he hummed merrily and said: "It is an enchanted life that we have my friend." And with those words he fell into a deep and peaceful sleep.

## The Wedding

Rodolpho chose his finest clothes for the wedding. As it was a cool and beautiful morning in May, and so, he wore a short scarlet coat with deep blue lapels over his off-white blouse and beige trousers. A gold embroidered Tyrolean blue cap, plumed with red and white feathers within the chorded brim sat upon his head and accented his fine features and flaming red hair which was wavy and long. He cut the perfect figure of a rustic squire accompanied by his beautifully groomed white companion, Netto.

It was just a short walk to the Church, but it took Rodolpho more time than he could have imagined as he was swarmed by well-wishers as he promenaded down the street past the smiling faces and waving handkerchiefs as would a victorious general, a king, or perhaps, even the Pope himself.

The small church was crowded with onlookers, gossips and busybodies alike, and of course, the young men of the village, whose hearts ached at the sight of their beloved Ginevra about to be married to some other. It was more than unkind that she should choose a foreigner from the North, possibly of German blood, rather than that of an Italian!

Like a Princess from a fairy tale she walked between the throngs outside and somber guests of family and dignitaries within the chapel. There was the exaggerated wailing of the women and the "shushing" by their husbands, but as she ascended the steps of the altar to meet her handsome betrothed, not a whisper could be heard. It was so quiet that a pin falling on the marble floor would have made such a terrific commotion not unlike a tree falling in a forest.

The beautiful colors projected from the stained glass above, created a mystical aura around the couple. Father Michele, the fat and jolly parish priest, cast a benevolent smile on them as he performed the marriage ritual. Would there be anyone to oppose the union? If it were so, then there was no one brave enough to speak out. The marriage was pronounced and the two kissed for the very first time. Rodolpho, now Roberto Da Veneto, the son-in-law of the Mayor of L'Aquila was rich and well married to the most beautiful woman in Italy, or perhaps, even the world!

As expected, the wine flowed, the people danced, and the presents were brought forth. A small boy brought the present which Rodolpho had forgotten in his haste to bring to the town hall. Finally he would discover the contents of the present which he had left unopened until this moment. Ginevra was anxious as well. Did she select a present which would delight, if not please her new husband?

"My dear husband, it is my fondest hope that I have pleased you with this gift. I pray that it will give you happiness for all of our years together.

"My heart is filled with joy for I have you as my wife and that alone would bring me happiness. I am sure that there could not be any gift that you could give that would not bring me pleasure."

Ginevra smiled and begged him to open the package. He teased her, opening it slowly, but then throwing open the lid and casting it to the side like an excited child, the gift was revealed...it was a beautifully carved zampogna!

The zampogna was carved from the finest exotic wood with a stain almost the color of ebony, the bladder of the softest leather, and the thinnest metal reeds within that gave the instrument its shrill tones enabled it to be heard for miles around. On each of the drone pipes sat small and delicately carved angels. The chanter was topped in ivory and sat comfortably on the lips.

Never before had Rodolpho seen such a beautiful instrument! Tears of joy fell from his eyes as he held the zampogna in his hands while the beautiful Ginevra beseeched him to play. The crowd yelled "Roberto, play us a tune!" He wetted his lips, pursed them on the tip of the chanter, and began to play the plaintive notes of tunes he grew to love as a poor shepherd.

Note by note the music filled the air and resounded amongst the surrounding hills. The audience was captivated by its sweet sounds, and was lulled into a hypnotic trance. Rodolpho played as never before and Netto's ears could now hear his master's sweet music for the first time. Netto lay before his master's feet and kept rhythm with his wagging tail.

It was not long before a dark eyed red-haired beauty appeared among the happy crowd. She made her way toward the happy couple and as she stood before them, Rodolpho immediately ceased playing the zampogna.

"Why do you stop Roberto?" the villagers cried out.

"Play, play, do not stop!" cried the Mayor.

Despite their protestations, Rodolpho's hands ceased to move and his lips opened as if in horror. Standing before him was the woman he had pledged his love and life to … it was Rosa!

"Did you think that I would not discover your treachery Rodolpho?"

"Who is this Rodolpho of whom you speak?" Ginevra replied.

"It is your husband, of course" Rosa snapped back at the young bride.

"Surely you are mistaken. My husband is not the person you call Rodolpho. His name is Roberto and he is not from these parts!"

"He is Rodolpho to be sure. He pledged his love and forsook me for your fortune and beauty."

"Surely this is not true. Speak my husband. Is this woman mad or does she speak the truth?"

Rodolpho without the slightest hesitation declared that he was Roberto Da Veneto and not Rodolpho, his ugly cousin.

"Look at me" he laughed. "You all know Rodolpho; none of you knew me when I arrived. Do I resemble my cousin at all?

"No!" they laughed. "Rodolpho the ugly! Roberto the handsome! There can be no mistake!"

Rosa lifted her arms above her head and uttered strange words that made the sky darken and the ground shake beneath their feet. The people of the town trembled with fear and Father Michele made the sign of the cross upon his chest.

"Oh beautiful Ginevra, see the man whom you say is Roberto as he really is!" Rosa screamed. "See the man whose sweet music softened my heart. Will you love him as I have loved him in his true form?"

As she pointed her finger at Rodolpho, a mist enveloped him, but as it faded, Rodolpho's ears grew large, the soft waves of red hair straightened and were made coarse, and his hands were rough and callused. Ginevra beheld a stranger in her midst … Rodolpho was once again ugly as before.

Rosa changed as well. No longer was she the ravishing beauty that Rodolpho had loved, but the old crone thought to be the mother of Rosa; wrinkled, hunch backed, fierce and terrifying to behold.

"The Strega!" the crowd gasped while making the sign of the cross.

"Yes, I am the Strega of the mountains. Beware of my love and of my anger!" The Witch began to laugh loudly and flew into the air. She swooped over the village in a circle and then disappeared over the mountainside.

"Praise be to God for our deliverance!' proclaimed the good priest.

Ginevra cried hysterically. Was this ugly man to be her husband until the last of their days? The crowd seized poor Rodolpho and brought him before the Mayor whose anger could not be abated. "You are a fraud…a thief…one who has consorted with the Devil!" The poor shepherd was immediately thrown into the jail and awaited his fate.

The good Lord sent comfort to the false Rodolpho in the form of the goodly Father Michele. Rodolpho, terrified of what would become of him, recounted his story to Father Michele in the form of a confession, and received absolution. It was only through the intervention of this sensible padre that his life was spared.

"I find no fault with this poor and wretched creature" the priest argued. "He is a poor shepherd, pitiful in appearance, and bereft of friendship. Is he not the perfect victim of a wileful witch? Surely the least of us all is easily deceived. I say that we show mercy upon this man. There is not a man among you who would not have looked upon this transfiguration as a gift from God almighty rather that the curse of the Strega."

The marriage was declared invalid and the Mayor's fire had cooled. Since the beautiful Ginevra had not consummated the marriage, her maidenhood remained intact.

Rodolpho returned to his former life again, but this time was without regret. He once again roamed the mountainside with his flock, accompanied by his beautiful dog Netto. The dog had remained beautiful as his heart could not be false. If you have a dog then you know that what I speak of is the truth.

The shepherd Rodolpho was no longer poor. He had retained his wealth and became wealthier still. His generosity toward the less fortunate was well known. Once again his heart was pure, and though ugly once again, he still had fond memories of the time that he had been handsome. And so, the gift given to him by the beautiful Ginevra was cherished and the beautiful, sweet sounds of his zampogna echoed throughout the mountains. His heart was full of joy once again. He had lost his love, it was true, but it was better to have loved and lost it than never to have loved at all!

The Zampognaro finished his story… and I do believe that there was not a dry eye among the guests. I was surprised to find that our host was not immune to the sentiment and noticed a melancholic air about Mr. Cherry as he faced me.

"Have you become a believer now Mr. Sportin' Jack?"

Mr. Cherry resumed his position of Master of Ceremonies. "It is time for another yarn!" he bellowed like a ringside announcer. "Who of you would be next?"

## Chapter 6 - Puddleston

As the clock drew nearer to midnight there was none who stepped forward to tell a tale. The guests seemed to shy away from the spotlight imposed by the crackling flames of the hearth.

"Cleopatra" and her knight seemed to have developed affection for one another and an Indian chief, whom I believe to be of an eastern woodland tribe, was in deep conversation with a man dressed in colonial garb and wearing a powdered wig. These persons seemed more interested in one another and chatted along at a frenetic pace as if time for them was running out. The most incredible thing about their conversations was that they spoke in their own tongue and as I had stated previously, they understood one another.

I had consumed more of the beverage than I should have perhaps and was growing tired when Mr. Cherry approached me, and taking me by the arm, led me to a small table with three chairs.

"Mr. Sportin' Jack" he said in a low and serious voice, "I would like for you to meet the acquaintance of a friend of mine."

"Certainly" I responded with a slight slurring of the tongue.

"My friend is a learned man, unlike meself. He is coming now. Let us take a seat and talk, shall we?"

We were led to the table by a short and quite rotund man, carrying a plate in one hand with a mound of food upon it, and a mug of punch in the other. He made his way slowly and cautiously through the throng of revelers least he should lose his supper in a collision with one of them. As he came closer he politely excused himself and sat down with his meal and began to eat.

"Please sit down gentleman" he mumbled, his mouth stuffed with food and directing us to our seats with a wave of his fork. Each portion was stuffed it into his mouth as if he had been a man starved for several days. He began chewing, and chewing until the tiniest morsel had been consumed before he attempted to utter another word. Then, taking a great draught from his mug, he stared upward a little as if he were to give grace to God; he shifted curiously in his chair. The worst and most repulsive behavior ensued. This strange man let go the loudest and longest belch that I have ever heard in my life before, and to be honest, have not heard since.

"Excuse me gentlemen if you consider my actions to be rude, but it is, to the contrary, considered quite unacceptable in many of the eastern principalities if the diner does not complement the chef with a hardy eructation…a habit that I have picked up while traveling in the Holy Land, quite beneficial for expelling that bloated feeling one gets after a enjoying a large meal. Wouldn't you agree?"

The ridiculous expression on the face of this man turned my mute revulsion into fits of laughter which I could not contain due to my consumption of the spirits in my mug. Mr. Cherry's strange laugh, which sounded like a horse whinnying, was so infectious that all three of us burst our sides in joyful merriment.

Mr. Chester Puddleston, whose recent acquaintance had given me such a low opinion on first meeting with him, turned out to be a queer, but remarkably intelligent man whose education and sense of adventure gave him the ability to perform magnificently as a raconteur.

His physique, being short and fat, gave the viewer no indication that this was a man who climbed pyramids, traversed jungles, and swam from a sinking ship torpedoed by a U-boat. His wiry red hair, which was sparse on the top of his head, stuck out from his temples, gave the appearance of a man receiving a perpetual electric shock. The hair was constantly raked with the fingers of his left hand, perhaps with the intent of flattening it. Of course, this proved useless as the static electricity caused it to stand on end. His eyes were pale blue, skin as white as a ghost, a small button for a nose, and lips, large and pink. In fact, Mr. Puddleston looked more like an overgrown baby than a man.

After Puddleston finished devouring his meal completely, he made his way to the front door. There were oohs and aahs from our guests which I took to be fearful. He reached for something next to the door which proved to be a brown leather valise of a much older style than I recognized.

"Well Gentlemen, here in my bag of goodies, I do believe I have an artifact that will make sense of all the mystery surrounding this house of spirits that we inherited."

"Inherited?" I enquired.

The subject was interrupted by Mr. Cherry, who corrected Puddleston's assumption. "Chester, my dear friend, Mr. Sportin' Jack…"

"John Francis Doherty" I offered with my hand extended.

"Mr. Doherty is a guest of ours tonight. Only the outcome of our endeavors may lead him to become part of our "Junto" if you will."

"Beg pardon, Mr. Doherty" he replied, taking my hand, but not before wiping it clean on his pant leg. "Latimer and I have not spoken for a fortnight when I received his letter of intent to contact you. You are a believer?"

I answered in the negative, but allowed that my interest had surely grown throughout the course of the evening. My initial fright had subsided (perhaps by the strong drink I consumed) but I now had many more questions than answers. "Mr. Puddleston, could you elucidate me in regards to our meeting?"

"Yes, yes, of course! Please call me Chester. May I call you Jack?"

I answered in the affirmative which brought a great smile from this odd little man that made his cheeks flush to a bright pink. He was quick to give me a little background on his education and expertise in all things related to Spiritualism associated with his studies in archeology. He exclaimed that he was by profession an antiquarian, that is, a person who studies or collects antiques or antiquities. His zest for knowledge in this field caused him to traverse the known world travelling by every conveyance possible to reach his destination whether by boat, train, coach, horse, or by foot.

Puddleston's social pedigree allowed him to finance his explorations, but not in a grand style that most persons of his class were accustomed too. He was a Yankee, from a long lineage dating back to the earliest settlers of New England. Though he was not roughhewn as were his ancestors, he nevertheless shared their sense of adventure and the hardships that accompanied it.

He kept a small shop in Newark, New Jersey where he was well known to those who were followers of that new phenomenon called the Spiritualist movement. Unlike the charlatans who plied their trade by duping people out of their hard earned money to communicate with their departed loved ones, Puddleston was a skeptic who investigated these claims and never charged for his efforts. As he was wealthy, to which degree I do not know, his was rewarded by the knowledge he desperately sought in acquiring truth alone.

It was through his place of business that Mr. Chester Puddleston had met the acquaintance of Mr. Latimer Cherry, and, it was through his grief from losing his beloved wife and two sons in the terrible disaster of the Empress of Ireland that Mr. Cherry, now a confirmed Spiritualist, sought the guidance of Puddleston.

RMS Empress of Ireland was a Scottish built ocean liner that sank near the mouth of the Saint Lawrence River in Canada following a collision in thick fog with the Norwegian collier Storstad in the early hours of 29 May 1914. In total there were 1,057 passengers on board the Empress of Ireland, included 138 children. Aboard the ship were 170 members of the Salvation Army, on their way to London for a conference. 840 passengers died, 217 survived.

Mr. Cherry was en route to New York for his business affairs after bidding his wife Ruth and sons, Vincent and Andre, goodbye in Quebec City. After enduring hardships for many years, Mr. Cherry's prospects were finally turning for the better but a twist of fate would shatter his dreams forever when he received the news of the ship's demise.

"How could God desert me?" he cried out in grief. "Ruth had given service to you her whole life. The boys would have proved valuable service in your name!" Cherry, formerly dissolute with drink, had been saved by no other than his future wife years ago. He swore off alcohol, and with Ruth's loving guidance became industrious. The two were eventually married later in life but were blessed with the addition of the two boys. All were active in the Salvation Army and were excited at the prospect of journeying to England to meet with other members in conference.

Cherry began to drink once again to soothe his grief but to no avail. He cursed himself and God almighty. His business prospects no longer interested him. The tortured man heeded no advice and forsook the charity and society of his friends. He no longer feared eternal damnation. His hell was on earth and he desired it now more than ever, but someone would change his life forever without saying a word by merely slipping a piece of paper into his pocket while he slept.

Upon awakening the next morning following his usual night of drunken self-pity, Latimer Cherry reached into his coat searching for the smallest amount of change necessary to put the "hair on the dog". He searched each pocket until he came to the last where he felt the unmistakable texture of paper. Thinking that he might have found a dollar inside, he smiled and whipped the paper out and into the light. To his chagrin, it was not money, but merely a small piece of paper folded in half. Irritated by his misfortune, the big man began to tear it when he noticed that it was a handwritten note in a beautiful cursive hand. He rubbed his bleary eyes and squinted to read the message. It read:

> ***You are cordially invited to attend a service
> at the United Spiritualists Church located
> at 244 W 54th St at 7 PM. Refreshments
> will be served. No Admission fee required.
> Donations are free will.***

Cherry was bemused by the invitation and muttered to himself: "Free will donation? I have none to give, but a free meal is one that I'd be willing to walk the distance for."

## <u>Chapter 7 - The Spiritualists</u>

I think it would be prudent to enlighten the reader with a short history of the Spiritualist movement, that being an integral part of my story, before proceeding to Mr. Latimer Cherry's introduction to the Spiritualists and his subsequent partnering, with Mr. Chester Puddleston.

Spiritualism, to be concise, is the belief that the dead can and do communicate with the living. The Afterlife, as had been presumed, was not the repository of souls, but rather a different dimension if you will, of its evolution. There is the belief that certain persons have evolved to a place among the living who have the ability to contact, send and receive messages from this netherworld. Of course most are charlatans preying on the misery of those who have lost loved ones and would spend any amount of money to parley with them once again.

The Spiritualist movement in America is relatively a newcomer amongst other religions. Its members are mainly composed of followers in English speaking countries. It peaked in the latter half of the 19th century and has, after the devastation caused by the Great War gained renewed interest and remains popular among the upper classes. Of course there are skeptics (myself included) who attempt to scientifically measure and quantify souls by meticulously studying the composition of the ectoplasm, or the earthly remnants following the completion of contact with a spirit through a séance.

Tricks of the trade, speaking horns, levitating tables, and mannequins dressed in ghostly attire are quickly outed, but the most shrewd and devious of the mediums have employed technology to enhance their deception with phonographs and electric lines connected to hidden microphones and speakers. Nonetheless, there have been mediums of high distinction, for example, Lady Arthur Conan Doyle, wife of that celebrated author of the Sherlock Holmes mysteries, who are beyond reproach as their sincerity is never in doubt.

The Spiritualists have declared March 31, 1848, as the date of the beginning of their movement. Sisters Kate and Margaret Fox, of Hydesville, New York, claimed to have made contact with a spirit. It was later claimed to be the spirit of a murdered peddler whose body was found in the house, though no record of such a person was ever found. The Fox sisters also claimed that the spirit was said to have communicated through rapping noises, audible to onlookers. The evidence of the senses appealed to practically-minded Americans, and the Fox sisters became a sensation. They had become the first celebrity mediums and quickly became famous for their public séances in New York, but in 1888 the Fox sisters admitted that this "contact" with the spirit was a hoax. For reasons known only to them, they soon recanted that admission.

"They might be a bunch of lunatics" Latimer Cherry chortled, "but my stomach is growling and a drink or two will settle this head of mine." He approached the house and was surprised to see that he was welcome. There was a large room with people of all shapes and sizes buzzing about and chatting it up with one another. He tried to be inconspicuous by removing his hat and overcoat, but being such a tall and large man he soon drew the attention of the hostess of the meeting, a Mrs. Blanche Asquith. She was an older woman, quite physically attractive for a woman of her age. Mrs. Asquith was a petite woman standing just over five feet in height. Her blonde hair and bright blue eyes contrasted with her elegantly tailored dark dress accented with the most elegant and tasteful complement of jewelry.

"Ah… Mr. Cherry. So good of you to come tonight…will you have something to eat?"

"Yes, thank you' he responded.

"And of course, we have refreshments as well. I do apologize, but there is nothing with spirits in them. You see, we Spiritualists do abide by the law."

Despite his disappointment, Mr. Cherry graciously thanked Mrs. Asquith and decided that he would eat his fill and make a quick exit towards the door when he thought to himself: "How did she know my name?"

With this thought going round in his head, Cherry searched each face in the room looking for one that might be familiar to him. He knew not a one! The food, as it turned out, was delicious, and he helped himself to several plates. The refreshments, all made from concoctions of various fruits wetted his palate. The combination of food and drink settled the fog in his brain and he began to listen to each of the members who in turn went to a podium and spoke to those seated in attendance.

As he listened to stories of loved ones lost he remembered his wife and children and began to bite his lip lest he let out a cry. Tears welled in his eyes as he thought that he would never see them again. His anger had made him proud. His pride had hardened his heart, but though he did not believe, he desired it more than anything in the world. You see, those who had lost their loved ones no longer despaired. According to the Spiritualists there was communication with those who had passed through, not merely passed away. The world unknown to the living could be breached through certain passageways called "portals". These testimonials began to tear away the wall surrounding Mr. Cherry's broken heart. There was joy to be had in the final destination, he was told, but as there was so much to be gained; there was danger in the journey.

Latimer Cherry stayed until the end of the meeting desiring to inquire of Mrs. Asquith, how she was able to know of him. Her demeanor, formerly cheerful and light, became more subdued and thoughtful.

"Please Mr. Cherry, let us have a cup of coffee and chat for a bit. Be mindful of that which I tell you. I am only a messenger, and the request that you come tonight had been passed on through a medium. A spirit requested that you be invited tonight. The spirit described you and where we could find you. I know nothing more, but you can speak with a friend of ours, a very kind and generous man who would be willing to help you in your quest." The address given to him was none other than that of Mr. Chester Puddleston, 13 Van Buren Street, Newark New Jersey.

Mr. Cherry made the acquaintance of Mr. Puddleston on the morning of November 13th, 1915. It is only worth mentioning because it also coincided with the birthday of Mrs. Cherry, whose memory was cherished by her grieving spouse. Mr. Puddleston, however, related the first meeting as somewhat frightening as he beheld the hulking shadow of this giant of a man standing on the stoop knocking loudly on the thick wooden door.

"I thought that the wolf was at the door" he recalled with a laugh. "I knew not what to expect and feared bodily harm!"

"Ah Chester, it is not right to judge a book by the cover?" Mr. Cherry chortled.

"A book can do one no harm, but a man can. Wouldn't you agree Mr. Sportin' Jack?"

"Of course", I nodded in agreement. The two men met in the parlor situated next to the hallway and discussed the contents of a letter in the possession of Puddleston.

"Mr. Cherry" he began. "I have been in the habit of attending séances for some time, not as a believer, you understand, but as a skeptic intent on unveiling the fraudulence perpetrated on grieving members of departed loved ones. I attended one of these séances by a well-known medium, a Madame Zulov. No doubt you have heard of her."

Mr. Cherry replied that he knew of the woman. Madame Zulov had recently become a popular celebrity known for her habit of wearing exotic eastern dress, heavy eyeliner, and topped her plump physique with a feathered turban which gave her the appearance of a fancy perfume bottle. Wherever she went, the local newsmen were sure to follow and quote her. Her mastery of theatre was evident. She spoke in long drawn out sentences and alluded to her royal Bohemian pedigree, which could not be verified. Nevertheless, this crafty woman was able to convince her followers that she was, indeed, clairvoyant, and the stories told by witnesses of her parlances with the dead captivated readers tired of the carnage of the Great War.

"And do you believe her?" Cherry asked.

"That is the reason that I have asked for you to be invited to the Spiritualist meeting. Mrs. Asquith was kind enough to direct you to my address, though I was uncertain that you would come. It seems that Madame Zulov was conducting one of her meetings with the departed complete with all of the theatrics associated with a séance, when one of the "spirits" entered the conversation. It was a woman who claimed to be your wife…I wouldn't have put much faith in it to be quite honest with you, but it seems Madame Zulov was noticeable shaken up by unexpected presence ... in fact, she fainted! You see, writing from an invisible hand began to appear in the middle of the tablecloth. I was able to remove a piece of it before Madame Zulov could regain her senses. I believe the woman to be a charlatan, but I saw the writing with my own eyes and I needed proof of its authenticity. Mr. Puddleston handed the note to Mr. Cherry. He read it, put his hand to his face, and cried.

"This is the address of the home where I reside …written in her hand… Mr. Puddleston … how can I ever repay you?"

"Mr. Cherry" he replied. "You just have repaid me more than the greatest treasure ever known. Now, though I am not truly a believer, I would like to get closer to the truth… with your assistance"

## **Chapter 8 - A Witchin' Moon**

As the time drew near to midnight a feeling of sadness was pervasive in the air. Guests embraced one another as if they were leaving on a long journey, perhaps never to meet again. A pair of disconsolate lovers gave a parting kiss, and Mr. Cherry turned in his chair searching the room for something. "Was he too looking for his family?" I thought. He turned toward us once again. The three of us sat in silence.

Suddenly the clock began to chime. One, two, three it rang. Four, five, six… the room began to darken … seven, eight, nine, ten, eleven …twelve O'clock. Then there was no one save myself and my companions. The guests had disappeared yet no one left through the door.

"Gentlemen…!" - I cried. "Not a soul has remained. Where have they gone?"

"Perhaps "they" have gone back to their home, of course" Puddleston replied with a "matter of fact" tone.

"Home…? Where pray God, is that?"

"If only we knew. I would join them."

"Latimer, we must not wish for an early departure from this world. We have much to do and I, for one, am not ready to leave until my curiosity has been satiated."

"As if it ever could be satiated Chester…?"

The response drew a chuckle from Puddleston. I was still somewhat shocked at the sudden disappearance of our guests. The fire was going out and I quickly gathered more wood by the side of the hearth. A roaring fire was once again giving birth to glowing embers in the hearth. The chill had not quite left me so I stood before its heat and watched its flames lick at the iron dog beneath.

As for those leaving us, this was witnessed by Mr. Cherry and I alone. Puddleston, though disappointed, was unable to observe the "guests" who attended the annual ghost club festivities. I was informed that because he did not truly believe, Mr. Puddleston was unable to see them. Could I have been a true believer, or had my mind been deceived?

"Well Jack, do *you* believe now?"

"Mr. Cherry, I must admit that I *do* believe that I am interested in learning more. Perhaps you can enlighten me about this "Witchin' Moon" of which you have spoken."

"I will be glad to tell you of what I know Jack. This moon is one that comes every 20 years or so. It's quite large as you can see" he said as he tapped on the window pane. "The local Indians, the Delaware people and the Leni Lenape relate that strange forces come together during this event. We Spiritualists believe that this event may act as a bridge, no, a corridor between our world and that which is inhabited by those who have passed over. The "Ghost Club" I'm afraid was a ruse to get you to come and join us in our investigation. There is no annual event but rather proof that the time was ripe with spiritual activity this time of year."

"What do you believe Mr. Puddleston?"

"I couldn't tell you Jack, my boy. I'm here to investigate. You see, as a man of science I have my suspicions and doubts, but I have developed a hypothesis of what may have occurred. Documents in regards to Johannes Kelpius, the sixteenth century mystic who immigrated to Germantown near Philadelphia have come into my possession. I intend to use them to try to solve this enigmatic puzzle."

"I've heard of Kelpius. Isn't he the leader of the doomsday cult; the hermit who lived in a cave?"

"Precisely... Kelpius, a German by birth, emigrated from the Transylvania region seeking religious tolerance. Philadelphia, which was founded in 1682, was like a beacon of light drawing enlightened men toward it. By all accounts, Kelpius was a gifted musician and writer with a keen interest in botany and astronomy, but that which interests me the most is his studies of the occult. Not that he was an evil man, he was quite religious, a pietist if you will. He predicted that the world would end in 1694..."

"Not too good on his predictions I'd say"

"Quite right Jack, but he gathered a small group that followed him to America. They lived and worked in a community and inhabited caves around the Wissahickon Creek. I can't say for sure if they were disappointed when the world did not end, but they seemed to disband after Kelpius'" death in 1708."

"But, what does this have to do with some cave dwelling loony?"

"Well ... this is where it gets interesting Jack. One of his disciples, a Wilhelm Guttmann seems to have continued on in his quest for purity. As more and more people immigrated to Philadelphia, animosity grew against the cultists, particularly Kelpius's German countryman. He was considered an odd duck, you see, and his unorthodox lifestyle of aestheticism seemed to make them fearful for their children."

"Was he one of those preachy types?" I inquired.

"Could have been...I don't have any documentation concerning evangelizing, but he was quite popular among the Indians who recounted tales of him talking with the dead."

"You mean that Guttmann was a medium?"

"I couldn't say for sure, but before he came to the area in which we are staying tonight, there had been strange goings on that scared the "begeebers" out of them. Guttmann was said to have been their savior. They took a liking to this strange man who ate no meat, had no woman, and lived in a cave. It seems that he quelled whatever evil spirits haunted them. In fact, he was held in such high esteem by the Indians, who took no liking to the white man's religion, that they lined up for baptism."

I was still befuddled. "What was the reason for my invitation?" I thought. Surely after all that I had experienced that evening I had become a believer in ghosts. The howling and tormented screams that filled the air outside filled me with so much fear that I dared not leave until the morning light, and even with much trepidation.

"Jack… let me explain. Mr. Cherry and I have found this house to be abundant with spiritual energy. We do believe that we have found a sort of "portal" between the worlds in which we inhabit with that of those who have passed through. It also seems strangely to be a "sanctuary" that the witches can approach but may not enter. We must of course stay the night, but with the first light of dawn we intend to investigate the area, with your presence being essential, as we plan tomorrow night to have a séance."

"I wholeheartedly support this enterprise gentleman" I responded with a newly imbued sense of adventure in my gut. "But we have no medium."

"I assure you that a medium is merely one who opens himself to a spirit guide. It must be someone who truly believes."

"But, Mr. Puddleston, I am still skeptical, and you, are you not a skeptic?"

"It's not me Jack. Someday I hope to believe, but as a scientific man I need physical proof."

Mr. Cherry stood up and walked to the hearth, tipped his stovepipe hat back toward the crown of his head and sighed: "I have no choice but to believe. I am your man!"

Puddleston, Cherry and I began to pore over all documents pertaining to this house which our antiquarian had managed to obtain. It is quite old, the earliest structure having been built in 1732 by a substantive farmer, a John Cooper. Subsequent additions have been built; small rooms including a kitchen, upper dorms, and what seems to have been a root cellar, initially in the rear of the original structure, but now accessible through the basement. Records from that time have been scanty at best, but there seems to be multiple owners from that time till now. There are at present no inhabitants and the house is in need of repair, but the structure is sound.

We intend to do a complete investigation of the house which Puddleston and I agree is necessary to rule out any tampering by special tricks used by unscrupulous locals to enhance the reputation of the house as being "haunted". This of course would lower the price of the property significantly for a land speculator interested in its key location between successful farms and close to Philadelphia.

As we discussed the history of the "Cooper" farm, as we now referred to it, great winds blew outside scattering leaves and other debris up into the air. These shapes coalesced and diffused in spectacular formations, silhouetted against the full moon, and marvelous to behold. It was not, however, a totally pleasant experience. My companions warned me not to leave the safely of the house though nature was calling me to relieve myself. The thought of indoor plumbing had never occurred to the owners, and so, I relied on my army experience to provide relief with the aid of a pickle jar.

Thanks to Mr. Cherry's good sense, we were well provisioned with food, drink, and firewood. The hearth was, and remains, the only source of heating. There is no electricity, so we relied on the light from two oil lamps placed strategically in the main room, and of course, the hearth. As my sleeping bag was still in my motorcar I was happy to have received one of the blankets provided by Mr. Cherry, who had been residing here for the last week. Though it was inadequate for this especially cold night, I managed to situate myself close enough to the fire to keep off the shivers. So, after several minutes of tossing and turning in an effort to find a comfortable position, I dozed off into a fitful sleep, filled with dreams of nightmarish manifestations of witches, demons and other hobgoblins.

## <u>Sybil</u>

I awoke the next morning to the splendid aroma of coffee brewing on the hearth. Cherry and Puddleston were huddled close to the fire preparing breakfast. Mr. Cherry's poker looked like a lance thrust through multiple sausages and Puddleston was in the process of cracking several eggs into a frying pan. A loaf of bread sat on the table to complement our breakfast.

The discomfort that I had endured the previous night awakened old aches and pains that I had sustained from former athletic injuries. The kink in my neck was so painful that I felt as one who had swung from the gallows. I tried to disguise my present state with a cheerful smile but the loud cracking sound coming from my limbs revealed the truth.

"Pleasant night?" inquired Mr. Puddleston.

"Slept like a baby!" I lied.

"Oh, that is wonderful. Mr. Cherry and I had the most unpleasant time trying to get comfortable. A hearty breakfast and a good stretch of the legs should get us back in fine form … wouldn't you agree Latimer."

"I was unaware that you had ever been in fine form Chester" Mr. Cherry replied with a smirk on his face.

"Hmm… well then… Jack, after breakfast I would like to do a little investigating around the area. Any place that you would like to start?"

"I should say so … gentlemen, but first, my motorcar is in a ditch a little ways down the road. I would be grateful to you both if we could retrieve it. I have provisions in it that would make our stay even more comfortable."

"By all means my boy, Latimer and I would be glad to pull your car out. It would be good to get these muscles a good go. Don't you think Latimer?"

Mr. Cherry beheld the fat little man with arms as strong as cooked spaghetti, smiled benevolently and nodded in agreement. Within minutes breakfast was ready and we filled our bellies with a nutritious meal topped off by the best coffee that I have ever tasted in my life!

After we had breakfasted, we three strode like gallant musketeers down the path that had terrified me the night before. There was evidence of having been strong winds by the debris which was scattered before us. Several small branches had to be kicked to the side having impeded our progress. I saw one large heavy branch sticking out of the ravine in the vicinity of my "Lizzie" and my heart raced as I ran toward it hoping that it did no hurt to my vehicle. I breathed a sigh of relief as I saw the motorcar was unscathed, the branch just missing the right front fender by mere inches. The three of us were able to right my Lizzie but if not for the prodigious strength of our amicable giant, Mr. Cherry, I do not believe we would have accomplished our task without multiple efforts and enduring much soreness.

I was wiping my sweating hands when I had the strangest feeling of being observed by someone or something. Looking from side to side I beheld only my friends chatting to each other. Bending my head in skyward position revealed the source of my uneasiness. Seated on a limb high in an old oak tree was the largest crow that I have ever seen in my life. I am no ornithologist, to be sure, but it looked more like a turkey vulture than any crow I've ever seen! I estimated it to be near thirty inches in length. The great breadth of the wings was revealed as the bird stretched them in its preparation for flight, but it had a singularly evil look about it as it watched my movements from above that unnerved me. I picked up a stick and tossed it upward toward my antagonist, but it merely stared down at me as if mocking my agitation.

"We had better get back gentlemen. We have much to do and so little time." Puddleston urged.

I agreed and the three of us attempted to get into Lizzie, but it soon became apparent that there was no room for our colossus. Mr. Cherry was disappointed but quite good natured exclaiming: "It's a fine day for walking anyway."

My Lizzie sputtered as it crept up the small inclined road which led to the Cooper house. Mr. Cherry, with those long legs of his had kept good time due to my periodic deceleration in order to catch of glimpse of every suspicious looking crow. I felt now that I was being watched by all of them; they knew something that I did not. Thankfully the large crow that gave me such a fright had disappeared, or so I thought: "Good riddance!"

I decided to park my vehicle around the back of the house lest the local people might find it and examine it. The usual reticence of farmers always gave way when my sportin' gal came down the street. It was uncommon for me to appear aloof, but in this instance I had neither the time nor the energy to explain every little detail to an inquisitive rube. Mr. Puddleston was quite impressed by the vehicle and maybe not a little envious when he took his ride with me. He expressed a desire to take the wheel, but he, having no prior experience at driving a motorcar, had to be gently persuaded to wait for a more appropriate time when I could give him a lesson or two. To this he merely nodded in agreement.

We turned a corner onto an old dirt road that ended just behind the farmhouse. A small empty stable (very convenient) served to keep my Lizzie safe and sound from the elements. As I was in the process of backing my vehicle into the stable I spied a small woman with two white dogs step directly in my path. I stamped my foot on the brake immediately to avoid hitting her. Before I could utter a remonstrance for the woman's stupidity, Puddleston gleefully called out like an excited schoolboy: "Sybil!"

The little woman, accompanied by two white dogs of some Scottish breed, pulled her cap off of her head and revealed light colored hair pulled up tightly into a bun. Her nose, rather small and upturned, twitched like a little mouse causing her gold wire framed glasses to rise and fall with each twitch. She was dressed in black from head to toe resembling one of the crows mentioned earlier but not threatening in the least.

"Chester! I can't believe that you have come to join us" she shouted in her thin reedy voice.

"Sybil, I wouldn't miss it for the world. Let's get your things into the house. We'll put some tea on. I hope you brought some of those delicious scones that you are so famous for?"

"Oh posh, Chester! You know that I always bake them for you... and yes, I didn't forget the caraway seeds."

I believe that Puddleston forgot to introduce me to his lady friend due to his desire for the scones, so I made myself known to her. "Good Morning" I said while doffing my cap. "I'm Mr. Puddleston's guest from the Philadelphia Inquirer. My name is ..." but before I could get another word out of my mouth, the little woman babbled incessantly that she knew who I was, asked me how I liked the place, and most importantly … was I a believer?

"Oh Mr. Sportin' Jack, I read your column faithfully. I am such a fan! Keeping up with the high society? I can see that you are also the adventurous type. I think that you will be well satisfied with the things that you are about to see and experience tonight. The Witchin' Moon is at its peak…not scared are you?"

"Not at all … may I call you Sybil?"

"But of course! May I call you Jack?"

I told her that she may call me whatever she pleases. She was a kind woman and gave a person the sense that you had known her all of your life. Sybil put her hat back onto her little head, somewhat askew, took me by the arm and commenced into leading me back to the Cooper place with her little white dogs following directly behind. Puddleston huffed and puffed under the weight of her baggage while dutifully carrying them into the house.

"Ugh, this house is so dark and dusty. Open the windows and let some air in!" Miss Barnhardt blurted out. "You little doggies better stay out of Mommy's way. I have some sweeping to do. Honestly, how can you men live with this dirt?"

"But Sybil, we were just about to clean it when …"

"Rubbish! Move those chairs Chester so I can sweep away the dirt." The little woman swept all the way to the front door. She opened it and looked up into the face of a giant standing silently in front of her. It gave her such a shock that she fell into a swoon but was instantly brought to her feet by Mr. Cherry.

"I'm sorry to give you such a fright. I was gathering wood for the fire."

I believe that Sybil was embarrassed but gathered herself and demanded that he announce himself from now on … and to knock before entering. Suppressing my laughter was not easily accomplished, but I managed to do so and exclaimed: "This is our friend, Mr. Latimer Cherry, and I can attest that he is a *friendly* giant."

"Oh Mr. Cherry, do beg my pardon?" she said wiping her hands on her dress and extending her hand. "Chester had informed me that you would be coming, but I thought you to be a hired hand." Once again she realized that her words were well intended but stumbled clumsily out of her mouth. Puddleston quickly moved in to save the situation.

"Now that we are all acquainted, perhaps we can sit down to a cup of tea and some of Miss Barhardt's delicious scones?"

"I second that" I responded. Mr. Cherry mumbled something in agreement. Puddleston wiped the table clean and put a large kettle upon it. The tea was poured into mugs since that is all that we had to drink with, and a plate of scones with a slab of butter was placed in the center.

"Well, gentlemen" Sybil proclaimed. We'd better set our agenda for tonight's foray into the unknown, but before we do, it is important that we learn a little history. Contact with those who have passed through is generally safe, but there are spirits out there who are not so genial. They are troubled, angry, and perhaps vengeful.

"Are they capable of deceit as well?" I enquired.

"Yes, indeed" Sybil responded as she nonchalantly broke the remaining scone (they were as delicious as Puddleston claimed) in half and fed it to her dogs. "The spirits retain their conscience, mind you, and it would not be unreasonable to believe that they would still attempt deceive us into thinking that they were someone else. There is still a mystery to be solved here. You have heard stories about the fanatical hermit named Guttmann, but we haven't discussed the person who was his sworn enemy…"

"Long Meg ... the Witch" Puddleston interjected.

"The witch that chased me to the door …?" I asked.

"Can't be sure" Mr. Cherry replied with a slight grin that increased as he remembered my hasty reception at the door of the Cooper house. "It could be one from her coven, or perhaps the old girl herself. No one knows for sure what became of her … or Guttmann. The Indians tell tales of their battles with each other, but all the facts are lost in the legend. Nobody knows for sure. That's why Sybil is here. She's a folklorist with a bit of the scientist about her. Between her and Chester, they'd be the ones to be askin' the questions Jack. I'm just an ordinary chap, but a true believer if there ever was one."

**Note: I'd like to give the reader a little background on Miss Barnhart. You may have taken the opinion, given my brief description of her that she is a bit of an eccentric, a real character. Your assumption would be correct, but she is quite a remarkable woman. She is a historian with a keen scientific mind as well as a folklorist of renown, especially in regards to the early colonialist period. Many of the legends, as previously noted, were based on fact. It is for us to find the truth behind the story. It was thought that through this most unorthodox of means that we might find information unavailable through the gathering of physical artifacts alone.**

"Jack, would you be kind enough to hand me my traveling bag? It's directly behind you."

"Certainly!"… I reached behind me to discover a rather large carpet bag valise which was heavier than expected. A pain shot up my arm due to lifting the weight at such an awkward angle. I made a quick decision to defer to my left arm and ceremoniously delivered the bag and its contents to its owner.

As Sybil opened the bag, her two white furry companions positioned themselves on either side with expectations of a treat.

This she provided before shooing them away with a swipe of her hand. One by one she emptied the contents of her bag onto the table. There were papers of all sizes, some old, some personal notes written in Gregg shorthand, and bits and pieces of Indian artifacts made of leather, a bone, and a feather. One could only imagine what use would be made of them. Puddleston looked at them with an antiquarian's eye, making mental notes of each as she proffered them one by one.

## Chapter 9 - A Feather, a Bone, and a Little Tobacco

Puddleston and I took leave of our comfortable little room by the hearth and decided upon giving the Cooper house a good going over before attempting the séance that evening. It was a dusty and dirty job that began in the second floor of the old farmhouse down into its foundation. We searched for wires, phonographs, props, and any suspicious item that we might find to indicate trickery on the part of Mr. Cherry (of whom I suspected not a bit of duplicity in the least). I must admit that my fondness for Miss Barnhardt did not prevent me from suspecting her. After all, it would be advantageous for a successful outcome if it proved her point. We had searched high and low into each crack and crevice. The only thing that we did find was a former opening in the basement which had been walled up and plastered over. Surely without any entry to be made, we figured it to be an entrance to the old spring house that was no longer needed.

Sybil was busy upstairs instructing Mr. Cherry on the proper procedures to serve as Medium for the séance to be conducted that evening:

1. It would, of course take place at the stroke of Midnight when it was believed that spiritual activity was at its zenith.
2. It would take place in complete darkness. An unlit candle would be placed in the center of the table. Matches would be provided for the spirit to light it.
3. All must hold hands and not let them go until the session has ended. The strength of the true believer (Mr. Cherry) would be necessary to sustain the doubters.
4. A Spirit guide, Black Eagle had been purported to make contact with spiritualists who have entertained at the Cooper farm in the past.
5. A feather, a bone, and some tobacco were thought to entice Black Eagle to come forth.

The same instructions were given to me and Puddleston by our worthy friend Mr. Cherry as Miss Barnhardt hung on every word

eady to correct him if necessary. Her little bun at the top of her head bobbed up and down in agreement with his recounting of each detail.

"Now that we have settled the business, let us have a little supper" declared a famished Chester Puddleston.

We were fortunate to have enough victuals between us to put together a sumptuous meal. I furnished some canned goods, but due to circumstances beyond my control, was unable to provide the trout which would have been caught due to my fishing prowess. Mr. Cherry kept the fire going and watched the coffee provided by Puddleston (It was of the highest quality) to keep us alert. Miss Barnhart's bag was filled with foodstuff of all sorts and quantities. It is hard to believe that such a small woman could have carried that weight such a distance. Further conversation revealed that she had been taken there by her father's hired hand by way of a haywagon.

Our lunch was punctuated by conversation of the most interesting subjects. Puddleston, the most erudite of all, impressed us with his travels through geographic locations so remote that I had been unaware of their existence. Mr. Cherry, in his younger days, had worked aboard colliers plying their trade up and down the St. Lawrence. The weather that he encountered in the Great Lakes could be as treacherous as any ocean. Several times he thought that he would never live to set his foot upon dry land. He survived them all; his numerable pleadings to God had all been answered. I took notice that after finishing his story, he bowed his head and muttered under his breath: "but my family ... why?"

It had been quite obvious that the others had heard his lament as well. Miss Barnhardt, in a most judicious manner, managed to bring the subject back to the history of the area, most notably of the conflict between Wilhelm Guttmann and the nefarious villain known in this part of the country as "Long Meg". I, of course, was quite familiar with Guttmann and his connection to the mystic Kelpius through conversation with Puddleston, but he had never mentioned Long Meg before.

Whether she was a witch or not remained a source of speculation, but the fact that she was a murderer seemed to be agreed upon by both the Indian and the White man. Recorded testimonials of her proclivity for using an axe on her victims, surprising them from behind or overpowering the vulnerable, gave me great angst as Sybil described missing children being found hacked to pieces.

"Had she killed them in some sort of satanic ritual?" I asked.

"She did have her followers… highly probable I suppose. They gave her the name "Long Meg" due to her having unusually long limbs. The Indians say that she stood more than ten feet tall!"

"Well, that's highly unlikely" I interjected. "Well then… about her followers?"

"They call them a coven" Puddleston added. "Knowing what we know about witches, they gather together to perform ritual sacrifice for their Dark Lord, Satan."

"Maybe we could ask the old girl herself tonight" I joked.

"It's no laughing matter Jack" Sybil replied in a serious tone. "Who can know for sure what evil may be unleashed?"

Our conversation was broken by the sound of Sybil's two dogs barking down in that dark, dank basement. She rose out of her chair and hurried to the cellar steps like an attentive mother. I lit a lamp and we proceeded down those rickety wooden stairs to find them scratching at the very spot where we found the sealed opening in the wall.

"I think they may be on to something" Sybil said.

"What do you mean Sybil? A spring house, a wine cellar …?"

"Perhaps that is all there is Jack, but my little darlings are very sensitive to things that are imperceptible to humans. For example, animals know when a storm or an earthquake is about to occur before we can. They are hypersensitive. Yes, I believe that supernatural activity that takes place in this house has a reason, and that they can feel it. Something has to do with that wall. We must get behind it. Therein lays the key to the solution…"

I made a quip about the dogs being terriers, not bloodhounds, but Sybil was so absorbed in feeling about the edges of the plastered wall with her fingertips that I was completely ignored.

"Jack, bring the light closer … I can believe that there is something scratched into the plaster … words, yes …"

Sybil was correct, but they were no words that we could understand. They were more like hieroglyphs, symbols that appeared like concentric circles, stars, arrows and the sort. We were baffled and called for Puddleston who made his way down the steps cautiously hugging the wall as there was no bannister. Unfortunately, due to his corpulence, the last step gave way and made a terrific racket. His foot had gone completely through the rotted wood causing him to fall face forward. Luckily he broke his fall in time. Sybil was quick to render aid to Puddleston, who greatly appreciating the attention, dusted himself off and went quickly to work.

"These hieroglyphics as you call them are not words by any description" he remarked while adjusting his spectacles in a most authoritative manner. "It appears that these are merely Hex signs, but not like those which we commonly find to be mere decorations on barn to mean "abundance" in the form of rain or harvest. No, these are of a much older type. These are a meant to ward off *evil*."

Miss Barnhardt put her finger to her lips as if in contemplation. The dogs sniffed at the base of the wall which had evidently been eroded by years of neglect. "I know that I have it somewhere … yes, a tale of Long Meg that I collected from Indian lore some time ago. The Leni Lenape of this area claim that Meg would disappear into caves with her victims, which she devoured. It was impossible to catch her as caves were thought to be passages to the underworld which no Indian dared venture. Guttmann proposed that the caves be sealed in the hope that Meg would be trapped. Could this be the entrance to one of the caves? It's hard to know. Most had been opened to a number of schemers who pretended to find valuable minerals inside.

"Mostly garnets and schists in these areas" Puddleston remarked. "Some of these "speculators" made a good deal of money producing "fool's gold" and magnetite, claiming it to be silver, to gullible people who gave their hard earned money to fund mining operations. It wasn't long before they had found that their benefactor had fled with their money and never to be seen again."

I remember making a remark, like P.T. Barnum's immortal phrase "There's a sucker born every minute" but both were in a deep state of concentration looking closely at the hex signs for clues.

"Ah, there's a little bit of paint still visible here … it must have worn away over time. Eh, some of the plaster here is newer. It's lighter in color here and darker down at the bottom. I believe that someone has been trying to keep up with it, but the house has been unoccupied for some time now."

"Chester, I do believe that you are right. A parson was one of the last if not the last person to reside here. The folk around here said that when he came to live here he seemed okay, but that he became somewhat of a loony, telling stories about witches and goblins and the sort. Maybe he became obsessed with the stories. Perhaps he was the one who engraved the hex signs in the plaster?"

We had been downstairs for quite a while. I noticed the faint odor of rotten eggs. "Could there be sulfur behind the wall? The cave may have been a source for mining it" I thought. Above us we could hear the heavy footsteps of Mr. Cherry milling about. "It's about time that we get back to business". As we were about to make our way up the steps, we could hear movement which seemed to be coming from behind the wall.

"Probably mice … or maybe their flying cousins" I joked.

Puddleston walked over to the wall and placed his ear flat upon it. He turned to us with a white face and whispered "I think that I detect the sound of someone or something breathing!" Sybil immediately put her ear to the wall in an attempt to hear but was interrupted by one of her dogs who whined for a treat.

"Fiddlesticks!" she snapped. "I can't hear a thing with your whimpering … spoiled!"

Heavy footsteps moved once again, but this time toward the cellar door. It was Mr. Cherry who beckoned us for a late meal before the séance. Sybil and Puddleston hesitated for a moment, still listening close to hear something, but the dogs and I were famished and we made our way up the creaking stairs that groaned beneath with every step that I took.

## hapter 10 – Séance

After lunch which was provided by our host Mr. Cherry, we all retired for a nap, which was suggested by Miss Barnhardt. Two small quarters upstairs provided us with a place to sleep though the accommodations were hardly desirable. We offered Miss Barnhardt the room with a small bed. Puddleston and I made ourselves as comfortable as we could with sleeping bags and blankets on the floor. As I stared up at the ceiling I thought to myself: "Well, at least the cobwebs are not lacking in providing a spook's approval for decorating." I fell into a deep sleep that was haunted with visions of ghostly apparitions but sometime later that evening, I awoke to the sound of Mr. Cherry's voice calling us for a late dinner.

We chatted about the preparations for the séance reinvigorated by the splendid dinner prepared by Mr. Cherry. While we slumbered he was fishing for our meal. He took note of all that we said and muttered the instructions given to him by Miss Barnhardt. His demeanor was calm but gave one a feeling that he was preparing for a communique with his wife. I felt sorry for him as I did not expect him to have success in contacting spirits given that he was not an experienced medium, if, in fact, there was an honest one amongst them in that profession.

We secured a quill pen from Miss Barnhardt, some fine tobacco from myself, and oddly from Mr. Puddleston, a flute carved from a bone. Whether it was animal or, even human, I cannot say with any certainty. Mr. Cherry set a bottle of ink and paper on the table and declared: "What good is a pen without paper and ink?"

"What a splendid idea Latimer" Puddleston chortled with delight. "I do hope that the spirits write in a language that I can understand."

"If you cannot understand it my Dear Chester…" replied little Sybil. "… then we are all at a disadvantage."

I took note of Mr. Puddleston's reaction to be called "Dear Chester". His spirits were ebullient to say the least. After dinner was finished Puddleston offered to help with the dishes. As I consider myself to be a gentlemen, I offered as well but was informed by Miss Barnhardt that I was their guest and that she would not be a proper hostess by allowing me to wash dishes. Mr. Cherry and I sat contented by the fire accompanied by the two doggies. I shared my tobacco with him and he remarked about the quality of the American brands. As a proud American I agreed with him completely. Let it also be noted that there was a considerable amount of giggling and squeals of delight emanating from the kitchen.

As daylight dwindled into dusk there was a noticeable change in the temperature. The moon appeared red like the face of the sun rising from the East, but unlike the sun, it gave no warmth. "I'd better put some more wood on the fire" I suggested.

"I've set the wood on the porch" Mr. Cherry responded. "I didn't think it too wise to venture far to get it on a night like this.

"A black bear would be more afraid of you than you of they" I laughed.

"No, not of the biggest bear am I afraid. It's what might get in that I fear … something much worse than a bear or mountain lion."

"What on earth could that be?" I responded with a smirk on my face.

"Something neither alive nor dead Jack … something evil … malicious. Tonight could be providential or tragic. It is better that we take no chances. I will get wood for the fire now."

The wind started to pick up to such a feverish pitch that Mr. Cherry was wobbled a few times as he walked with his bundle. It was with some difficulty that I shut the door immediately after he returned. "I better bolt this door … maybe put something behind it" I joked.

"Let's hope that there isn't something already behind it on the other side" Mr. Cherry quipped. It is the first time that evening that I perceived some levity from our most admirable friend the entire day.

Wood was placed into the fire, and within minutes it seemed, the room heated up to a comfortable temperature. The face on the clock which was placed upon the mantle was illuminated by one of the lanterns. It was nearing eleven o'clock and we were rejoined by Sybil and Puddleston. The necessary objects were placed on the table for our foray into the unknown… Mr. Cherry solemnly placing the quill, ink, and paper directly in front of him. I pitied him knowing that he placed all of his hopes and dreams of contact with his beloved Ruthie, Vincent, and Andre in a vain attempt to communicate with their spirits, the bodies of which had never been recovered. I have only heard of one person actually coming back from the dead, our lord Jesus. You might argue that Lazarus and the daughter of Jarius also came back from the dead as well, but it was Christ who called them to him. The idea of a mere man being able to do what only God can do was simply preposterous to my way of thinking.

Tick, tick, tick ever closer to the hour of midnight brought a tingle, no, a sense of excitement growing within each of us. Perhaps there was a nervous apprehension on the part of our Medium but it was masked beneath that distinguished face. His hat when removed from his head revealed a curiously old fashioned styling of his hair, parted in the middle and sweeping backward and up into two peaks. As I looked across the table and noticed the resemblance that Puddleston had to Pickwick, I had the feeling that these two characters walked right out of a Dicken's novel. Perhaps Miss Barnhardt, with her sweet little face, apple cheeks and the old fashioned bun on the top of her head was the perfect companion for that queer little fellow, Mr. Chester Puddleston after all.

With minutes to go before the Witchin' hour we had assembled ourselves together at the table. Puddleston had managed to maneuver himself next to Sybil who was seated next to Mr. Cherry. So, there I set, one hand held by a giant, the other by a dwarf …admittedly, a very crafty one indeed.

The clock struck one, then two, then finally… twelve! We sat in silence; the unlit candle and hearth would be our only sources of light in the darkened room. The scent of my tobacco burning filled the air. Mr. Cherry began the séance with his voice *en basso profundo* calling out: "Black Eagle, we beseech you to guide us to the spirit world!" Alas there was no answer. Again he repeated his words but to no avail. I felt Cherry's grip tighten on my hand and hoped that it was not gripped so strongly on Miss Barhardt's tiny fingers.

In an act of desperation Mr. Cherry called out: "Black Eagle, I implore you to be merciful to a true believer. I implore you to guide us to the spirit world!"

Suddenly the candle was lit with no aid from any of us. It was then that I was shocked to behold the ghostly white spectre of an Indian hovering directly above Mr. Cherry's great head. It flittered just like the candle's flame.  I heard a small startled gasp emanate not from Miss Barnhardt, but rather from Puddleston. I turned to my right and saw his eyes popping out of his head. Cherry and Sybil sat with eyes closed unaware of the ghostly presence.

A voice came forth in what I could only describe as someone whispering loudly. The bony flute began to play softly in the style of an Indian flute. The music soothed the nerves of my gargantuan companion who then loosened his grip on my hand. He began to speak again:

"Are you Black Eagle?"

"It is I that you seek."

"Will you guide us in the spirit's world?'

The spirit gave it's response in the affirmative. Sybil began to question Black Eagle about Wilhelm Guttmann and inquired if he could reach him. Black eagle said that he knew him in life and that the two had met after passing through the portal to the next dimension. Guttmann, he professed, had been of a higher level of perfection than he and had ascended to a higher plane of existence.

Mr. Cherry beseeched the spirit guide to contact his wife and sons. He replied that "he knew them not". Cherry again begged for him to contact Ruth, his wife but the Indian's voice began to fade as he bid us a warning of "evil wears a false face". The spirit faded from view and at that point I believed that the séance was at an end, but Mr. Cherry moaned and called out in desperation: 'Ruthie, if you are there call out to me, your loving husband!"

To our surprise he was answered by the sound of a woman's voice responding to his plea: "Latimer, I am here!"

"Vincent … and Andre are there as well?"

"We are here and we wait … for you. We cannot reach you for the portal is sealed."

"Sealed… what can I do to *un*seal it?" he cried out.

"You must tear down the wall to the portal. It is in your power Latimer. Please release us from this torment. We long to be with you!"

Mr. Cherry released his grip and rose from the table and started toward the cellar. "No man!" Puddleston cried out. "You are being deceived! Black Eagle has given us warning to beware of the evil with the false face! Stop!"

The desperate man took no heed of our entreaties to desist. He took one of the lanterns and searched for something heavy to break down the wall. There hanging on the back wall of the pantry among the farming tools was a heavy pickaxe used for digging up large rocks.

The pick lay on his shoulder. He raised the lantern in front of him and barreled down the staircase breaking some of the steps with the force of his heavy boots. We pursued him while imploring him to stop this madness. What evil was behind that wall we knew not but the fear in my heart was palpable.

Each swing from the pick found its mark. A foul stench like rotten eggs emitted from the wall and permeated the little cellar. "Brimstone!" shouted Sybil. This is brimstone from the bowels of the evil one. Mr. Cherry, Latimer, please stop."

Sweat poured from his heavy face. He threw off his heavy coat and rolled back his sleeves. Dust flew everywhere. Whoever sealed this entrance surely made a good job of it, for after several minutes the wall was still standing with an opening the size of a fist. Cherry labored still. Sounds of something scurrying about behind the wall grew louder. Sybil feared that rats would scatter about the room in a frenzy fearing an attack by them. Sybil, to her credit, was wise enough to seek safety upstairs. Realizing that his efforts were useless, Puddleston turned round and followed Miss Barnhardt.

Cherry repeatedly hit the wall, stroke after stroke when suddenly a large gaping hole appeared. He leaned over to look in when he was confronted by a shocking sight. It was not Ruth that he released, but long Meg! Flames burned brightly in the deep recesses of where her eyes had been. The mouth was opened wide as if about to scream. The skin was gray and shriveled like that of a mummified corpse. But whatever this thing was … it was alive!

The big man wheeled backwards but not before a long limb with skeletal fingers gripped his throat. He tried in vain to release the grip with his powerful fingers. His face reddened, his lips were turning blue and just when I thought he was about to pass out I gathered my nerve and took the pickaxe in hand and brought down a crashing blow upon that evil arm causing it to sever and fall to the ground. This quick action, I believe, saved my friend's life, for if I had failed to act I am certain that he would have been killed.

Our moment of terror had not ended. While we gathered ourselves to guard from another attack, the severed arm dragged itself with its bony fingers with the intention of assaulting Cherry once again. Meg was pulling herself through the increasing gap in the wall with one hand while blackened forms reached from behind. It was at that moment that we took flight, and I am proud to say that I defended my friend in a manly way as he made his escape up the steps. Armed with my terrible weapon, I swung and hacked away at them as I retreated up the steps to the kitchen.

It was to their credit that Sybil and Puddleston pulled the curtains from the windows and proceeded to light them and place them at the top of the steps. As the flames grew we tossed the firewood and every conceivable item that would ignite easily. Smoke filled the rooms and we gasped for air. It was difficult to find the door with all the smoke rising, but we were able to crawl on the floor toward a window. Finding that it had become stuck I stood up and blindly struck with my axe   creating an exit with an explosion of shattered glass.

The smoke billowed out into the cold night air, but fearful that we should be cut exiting the house, I took up again with my pick and smashed the wooden frame and cleared away the remaining fragments of glass.

Despite our frenzied state of mind, all evacuated the house with not a single cut. The doggies were thrown like missiles by their owner first. They were unharmed but yelped as if injured. Puddleston heaved his lady through next and then, given a quick push by his friend Cherry exited as well. I stood for a moment expecting a rush at the door but the flames kept those "things" at bay.

As I was readying my own exit a curious event was caught from the corner of my eye. The table which we had in our haste forgotten to burn, sat unmolested by the all of the drama which had unfolded. The candle burned as before and to my amazement I witnessed the quill being dipped into the inkwell. It began to scribble something furiously on the paper and once again fell upon the surface. I momentarily forgot the peril that I was in and pounced upon the inscribed paper and tucked it away in my pocket before leaping through the window for safety.

Ghastly screams filled the sky as the house and the demons inside were completely engulfed in flames. It burned with such intensity as to be felt on our skin from quite a distance. We retreated to the barn to retrieve my "Lizzie". I started her up and in a minute Sybil, Puddleston, the dogs and I were barreling down the little road to escape the flames. Mr. Cherry's large frame was silhouetted by the orange glow behind him.

We three cheered aloud as we had all escaped, for certain, a most horrible destruction.

We huddled together in that little car to keep warm that night, but Mr. Cherry seemed to be impervious to the cold. I must have dozed a little because I was wakened by the sound of a rooster crowing. We wiped the sleep from our eyes and laughed once again as Mr. Cherry snored aloud, oblivious to everything around him.

After some time we made our way to the home of the Barnhardt family. As expected, they were all somewhat different than the local population, but warm and hospitable. The four of us huddled around the fireplace comparing notes as the two white doggies departed our company to chase squirrels, bunnies or perhaps the family cat. I had almost forgotten about the paper until I reached into my pocket for my pipe and tobacco.

There was the note, slightly discolored from the smoke but untouched by the fire. It was a poem addressed to Latimer. I looked at it but for a second and handed it to him to read.

To my beloved husband:

**Though winter's frost claim the Earth**
**And darkness cloak the light of day**

**Neither fear nor pain will trouble thee**
**Whilst thou lie sleeping**

**The withered flora lay in beds**
**Where in our youth we did play**
**And frolic with hearts full of glee**
**Never more...**
**Whilst thou lie sleeping**

**Cruel, the hand that took from me**
**The love the Lord bestowed with thee**
**I wait, till them, with sighs and weeping**
**Whilst thou lie sleeping**

**In my breast with heart a' broken**
**Yearning for thou yet awoken**
**And wish to embrace once again**
**When together... shall lie sleeping**

Tears welled in the eyes of Mr. Cherry as he read the paper. His suppressed cry choked up like a ball in his throat and he looked up at us with a smile on his face and said: "It is in the hand of my Ruthie. She always had the gift, but thought it silly to pursue it ... so humble she was, so delicate ... so caring. I can now have peace for the rest of my days. She is with me yet, and we will all meet again."

## pilogue: And What of Sportin' Jack?

We parted company that very day. I never saw Mr. Cherry again, but was happy in the knowledge that he had become active in the Spiritualist movement and found happiness again with the widow Mrs. Asquith. Some years later I was delighted to receive an invitation from Miss Barnhardt, who informed me that she was now known as Mrs. Puddleston and the mother of their two small children. I visited them one summer day in my new convertible accompanied by my fiancée, who like me had an interest in the spiritual world rather than the Spiritualist movement. I laughed heartily as I witnessed a decidedly thinner Mr. Puddleston chasing around after his little boy Latimer, and daughter Ruthie. Of course a litter of white Scottish terriers surrounded the little woman with the bun on the top of her head (now somewhat stout) who offered them treats while we enjoyed a leisurely lunch on that fine early summer afternoon.

My own life had changed dramatically on the day that I returned from my adventure to my home in Philadelphia. I was excited about the prospect of putting my story on the front page of the Inquirer, sure that my exploits of the prior day would excite my editor. Unfortunately for me, I had already been replaced by another "Sportin' Jack", whom I discovered was a blue blood relative of my boss, recently graduated from an Ivy League university. I protested of course, but was reminded that the personage that I had assumed was the creation and thus, the property of the Newspaper itself.

I was righteously indignant and demanded that my job be reinstated. Words flew, tempers flared and I became unusually hot under the collar. I controlled my temper as long as I could until the statement was made: "Go back to the bar where you belong with all your drunken Irish friends. You'll never work as a writer in this town again!"

My rage could not be contained this time. My Boss foolishly lunged at me with his heavy body and his fist high in the air. I responded instinctively, balled up my fist and sent it flying full force into his fat face, dropping him instantly.

Three policemen who had been nearby heard the fighting and appeared at the doorway.

"I want that Irish hoodlum arrested immediately!" my editor screamed as he was recovering his senses.

A smile grew on the lips of each of the officers. The fattest of them responded with a red face: "Now which of you would like to arrest Mr. Doherty? Would it be you Officer Murphy … perhaps Officer MacBride? It seems that without a witness we won't be arresting Mr. Doherty today" he said with a wink of the eye.

I never did work as a writer in Philly again, but I did write again. I hope that you have enjoyed reading this book and hope you will read my others as well.

-   Mr. John Francis Doherty.

# About the Author:

The Witchin' Moon is the sixth book and third novel written by Author and Illustrator T.R.Hart.

From his earliest memories the author had been fascinated by puppetry and scary stories. With skills learned as a museum preparator, Mr. Hart began to make puppets, and with his son Tommy, they performed puppet shows (*I Maccheroni Puppet Theatre)* together for audiences young and old. In this novel he combines Witchery with Ghostly apparitions, history with a dash or horror, and a little bit of comedy with mystery. A perfect recipe for a good read.

T.R.Hart is also the author of The **Adventures of Professor Saputello** books for children.

He resides in beautiful Lancaster County Pa. tucked away in the Amish Countryside, where he shares his life with the love of his life Ellen and their two West Highland Terriers, Ozzie and Snowy.

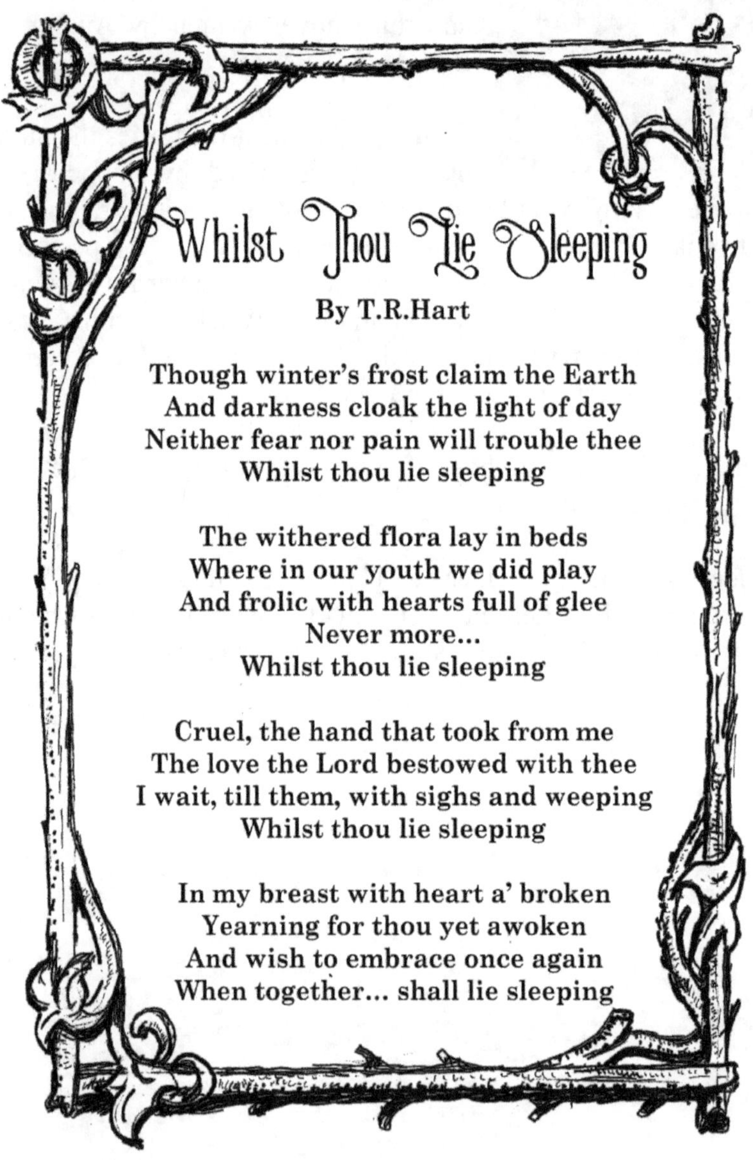

# Whilst Thou Lie Sleeping

### By T.R.Hart

Though winter's frost claim the Earth
And darkness cloak the light of day
Neither fear nor pain will trouble thee
Whilst thou lie sleeping

The withered flora lay in beds
Where in our youth we did play
And frolic with hearts full of glee
Never more...
Whilst thou lie sleeping

Cruel, the hand that took from me
The love the Lord bestowed with thee
I wait, till them, with sighs and weeping
Whilst thou lie sleeping

In my breast with heart a' broken
Yearning for thou yet awoken
And wish to embrace once again
When together... shall lie sleeping

More Books
by T.R.Hart

The Traveler

Ghostly Tales

Jack's Alive!

Terror Below!
&
The Adventures of
Professor Saputello